THE
WIZARD'S
DOG

THE
WIZARD'S
DOG

THE
WIZARD'S
DOG

Eric Kahn Gale

illustrated by Dave Phillips

CROWN BOOKS
FOR YOUNG READERS
NEW YORK

Text copyright © 2017 by Eric Kahn Gale
Jacket art and interior illustrations copyright © 2017 by Dave Phillips

All rights reserved. Published in the United States by
Crown Books for Young Readers, an imprint of Random House
Children's Books, a division of Penguin Random House LLC, New York.

Crown and the colophon are registered trademarks
of Penguin Random House LLC.

Visit us on the Web! randomhousekids.com

Educators and librarians, for a variety of teaching tools,
visit us at RHTeachersLibrarians.com

Library of Congress Cataloging-in-Publication Data
Names: Gale, Eric Kahn
Title: The wizard's dog / Eric Kahn Gale.
Description: New York : Crown Books for Young Readers, 2017. |
Summary: When his master and best friend, Merlin, is kidnapped, there is
nothing Nosewise the dog will not do to get Merlin back, even if it means
facing the strange Fae people and their magic-eating worms, or tangling with
the mysterious Sword in the Stone.
Identifiers: LCCN 2016008920 (print) | LCCN 2016028345 (ebook) |
ISBN 978-0-553-53736-9 (hardback) | ISBN 978-0-553-53737-6 (lib. bdg.) |
ISBN 978-0-553-53738-3 (ebook)
Subjects: | CYAC: Dogs—Fiction. | Magic—Fiction. | Merlin (Legendary
character)—Fiction. | Arthur, King—Fiction. | Fairies—Fiction. | Middle
Ages—Fiction. | BISAC: JUVENILE FICTION / Legends, Myths, Fables /
Arthurian. | JUVENILE FICTION / Animals / Dogs. | JUVENILE FICTION
/ Legends, Myths, Fables / General.
Classification: LCC PZ7.G13134 Wi 2017 (print) |
LCC PZ7.G13134 (ebook) | DDC [Fic]—dc23

Printed in the United States of America
10 9 8 7 6 5 4 3 2 1
First Edition

PART I

1

◈

Stupid Door

ALL DOGS HATE DOORS. THEY KEEP YOU INSIDE WHEN YOU WANT to go outside and outside when everyone else is inside. The front door blocks the garden, the kitchen door blocks the water bowl, and the pantry door blocks all the food a dog could ever eat.

But in my house, the worst was the study door.

Bangs, fizzles, pops, and whizzes sounded through the study door, perking my ears. My pack stayed behind the study door all day and kept me locked out. There was a small gap between the door and the floor, where I liked to stick my nose. I smelled burning grass, boiled bones, and sweet nectar.

What are they doing in there? I would wonder.

One hot summer day, I couldn't stand it anymore. I stood outside the study door and barked my loudest bark. "Woof!"

"Stop that, Nosewise!" I heard Merlin say on the other side.

I didn't like disobeying Merlin, but I was *bored!*

My claws slashed at the study door, tearing away splinters. I barked directly into the gap.

Stupid door.

The handle above me jiggled and turned. The door swung open, sucking air past my ears. The towering figure of my master, Merlin, stood before me. Long flowing robes rose up from his feet, passed knobby knees and a rounded belly, and finally disappeared under his bushy beard. His eyebrows arched and his long nose bent down at me.

Is he angry? I wondered.

"Nosewise," he said in a kind voice. He knelt and offered his hand. "Are you feeling abandoned?"

I pressed my forehead into his palm and wagged my tail shamelessly. A warm smile crossed his face.

"Master Merlin, now why'd you open the door?" a voice asked behind him. I looked up and saw my pack mate, Morgana, dangling a glowing stone from a chain. Her little face crinkled and she glanced at me.

When Merlin first brought me to his house in the woods, I found Morgana already living there. She was a little bit bigger than me, and definitely the favored pet. She knew all sorts of tricks like opening doors and getting food down from the pantry. She ate from a plate at the table like Merlin, never from a bowl on the floor. But why was she allowed behind the study door while I was stuck in the den?

"He's never gotten used to being separated from us," Merlin said, sighing.

"You're the one who wanted a dog," said Morgana. She

lowered the glowing stone and slipped it in her front pocket. "This is what a dog is like!"

"I've had dogs before, my dear girl. But never one quite as attentive as this."

"Well, maybe you should let him sit with us," Morgana said.

"Sit with us? While we *work?*"

"What harm could he do?"

I looked up at Merlin and wagged my tail.

"Oh ho ho! He knows that puppy face gets him things," Merlin said, laughing. "Come in before I realize what I'm doing."

I bounded into the study, the door swinging shut behind me. The air inside was rich with scents: fatty, acidic, moldy, ripe, metallic, sweet, and sour. Rows of tall wooden shelves lined the walls—they were stacked with hundreds of plants, dried animals, soils, and mysteries! My nose went wild with all I was smelling.

"Careful with the potion ingredients!" Morgana said as I scurried about. She tried to grab me with her tiny hands, but I dodged her.

"The ones on the bottom shelves are safe to sniff," Merlin said, smiling.

I found pollen, tree roots, fish scales, and oils I couldn't identify. A dish of pickled slugs caught my nose. I'd sampled some live ones I'd found in the garden, but nothing as tangy and sharp-smelling as these. I buried my snout in the pile and slurped them up.

"Nosewise, drop it!" Morgana grabbed me and stuck her fingers in my mouth. She tried to pry open my jaws. "This is disgusting!"

I swallowed the slugs, triumphant.

Morgana sighed and wiped her hands on her tunic. *If she wanted the slugs, she should've eaten them first!*

"Nosewise, come!" Merlin said firmly. I tensed and walked to him.

"Sit," Merlin said, pointing at the floor. I did as commanded, and he rubbed my head. "If you want to stay with us, you'll have to behave." He gave me a stern look, and I wagged my tail guiltily.

"Good boy," Merlin said, and looked up at Morgana. "Why don't you start where we last left off? You were channeling light from the stone."

Morgana took a short breath and pulled the silver chain out of her pocket. At the end was the little glowing rock. My ears perked up. I'd never seen anything like it before.

"I know it's silly," Morgana said, glancing at me, "but it makes me a little nervous to have Nosewise watch."

"Oh, you could have a worse audience than Nosewise." Merlin smiled and rubbed my head. "What if instead he was a knife-wielding bandit? Or worse, a grumpy old wizard like me?"

Morgana smiled and dangled the silver chain before her face. The stone on the end glimmered.

"Fix what you want in your Mind's Eye," Merlin said, pointing his finger in the air.

"A strong beam of light," Morgana answered.

"And do you have your Certainty?" Merlin asked.

"I do."

Morgana's eyebrows knitted together. She gnashed her teeth, and the glowing rock on the chain grew brighter.

Merlin gestured forcefully and gave her words of encouragement. It reminded me of the previous week, when Merlin had taught me how to Sit! He would point at the floor and repeat "Sit! Sit! Sit!" It was confusing at first. *Why is he pointing? And what's this word?*

But after some time it dawned on me: *butt down, nose up—that's Sit!* Merlin clapped and scratched my ears and gave me little chunks of cheese (my favorite) every time I would Sit! It felt so good to know a trick!

"Take the image and sit it down deep in the seat of your Mind's Eye," Merlin commanded.

Ah! There's the word! I thought.

Was he teaching her to Sit! as well? I'd seen her do it before but not on command. She looked nervous and a little bit frightened, just the way I felt when Merlin was teaching me! Oh, I hoped she would get it soon. She and I were pack mates, after all—once she'd learned, we could Sit! together.

"Strengthen it with your Certainty," Merlin growled. "Then send it out powerfully through your Asteria!"

"I—I will," Morgana stuttered back.

Sit! I thought. *Morgana, you can do it!*

"Go!" Merlin shouted. "Now! Release your Certainty!"

Morgana grunted, and the stone on the chain flashed brightly. A beam of light emerged from the center and sailed across the room like a firefly, then landed on a small writing desk.

Poof! It caught fire! Big flames fluttered up from the wooden desk and jumped to the shelves on the wall. Flowers and herbs blackened into oily smoke. I yipped and scrambled behind Merlin.

"A bit more control!" Merlin shouted, grabbing his staff off the wall. He pointed the handle at the flames, and I saw that a glowing stone was set there too, one I hadn't noticed before.

Pffff!

Freezing wind blew from it like a miniature blizzard.

The flaming desk and shelves instantly went out, extinguished by icicles that encased them.

My fear subsided. Excitement spread from my nose to my tail, waggling me from side to side.

Sit! was all right and all.

But I wanted to learn *that* trick.

2

The Other Apprentice

I FOLLOWED MERLIN AND MORGANA INTO THE STUDY EVERY morning after that and tried to understand all the strange things they said.

"I'm ready for Winter magic now, Master Merlin. Summer spells are behind me."

"An illusion spell can render a wizard invisible, or call forth the image of a monstrous beast!"

"I feel my Certainty faltering. How can I make it more powerful?"

I didn't have a clue what they were talking about, but I *knew* he was teaching her more tricks. Morgana brought fire and light out of the glowing stones. She made a small silver fox appear at the table. I barked at it, and it dissolved into a wisp of smoke. She mixed the things from the shelves together in pots and made smells I'd never sensed before.

Whenever she did something new, Merlin praised her.

He clapped his hands and did little dances with her across the floor.

All the amazing things Merlin taught Morgana to do were making me jealous. Sure, Merlin eventually taught me to Shake! and Lie down!, and I got treats and praise when I did them. But Merlin was only impressed for so long.

I'd follow him around the house, Sit!ting on my backside, raising my paw to Shake!, and Lie down!ing again and again. But Merlin stopped being impressed. "Very good, Nosewise," he'd say, giving me a quick pat on the head before heading to the study to teach Morgana something amazing. And how *could* I impress him? She made fire and ghostly animals, disappeared objects, and, most of all, opened doors!

At night I'd try the tricks I'd seen Merlin teach Morgana. Once, I tried to shoot lightning from my paws. How different was that from Shake!?

"Is something wrong?" Morgana said, watching me raise my paw again and again. I turned to her and grumbled; she was spoiling my concentration. "Maybe you want a treat," she said, fetching a bone from the mantel.

You're not supposed to get a treat until you do the trick! I thought. But I was never going to turn down a bone. *I'll definitely earn this next time!*

I tried to make leaves float, turn my food dish invisible, and open the front door with my nose. Nothing worked. It made me bark and whine.

Why could Morgana do those tricks while I couldn't? We both spent all day watching Merlin. We both were loyal pets. Morgana had hands for picking things up, which helped, but I was nearly as good with my mouth.

"May I see your Asteria?" Merlin said one day as he tutored Morgana. She opened her palm and offered him the glowing stone. It shone brighter when she dropped it into Merlin's hand.

"You shouldn't make direct contact," Merlin said. "I know it makes it easier to access the power, but it's harder to focus. That's why I keep mine in the handle of a staff."

"Your Asteria is more powerful," Morgana answered. "I need to hold it close to do what you do."

"The power does not reside in the stone," Merlin answered. He held the silver chain and let the stone dangle. It pulsed with light, like a heartbeat. "It merely brings into the world what lives inside you." Merlin pointed at the space between Morgana's eyebrows. "Cultivate what lives in your mind and the Asteria will bring it out."

The Asteria? I thought. *Is that what lets Morgana do the tricks I can't?* I hadn't paid much attention to the glowing stones, but there was something strange about them. In the first place, they glowed, which I didn't think stones normally did. But they also had a very special scent—one that made me feel all tingly on the back of my neck. Something special was happening there.

I jumped up onto a wooden chair and vaulted to the table in front of Morgana. She raised her eyebrows at me. "Hello, Nosewise," she said.

"Get him down from there," Merlin said over his shoulder as he walked to the shelves on the far side of the room. "I have a salve somewhere that should help you concentrate."

He turned away from us and went about his business. I padded to the edge of the table, my nails clicking on the wood, and reached my nose toward Morgana's closed hands. I sniffed and noticed (besides the scents of her skin and remnants of lunch) that *tingly* scent again. *What is that?* I wondered. It smelled like nothing I'd ever known.

"I don't understand this thing either," Morgana said to me quietly. She opened her hands and revealed the glimmering stone. As I sniffed, I felt a strange lightness in the corners of my mind. Something like a thought—but one I didn't recognize.

"Fancy it, do you?" Morgana asked. My ears perked up, and I glanced at her, whiskers twitching. Something odd was coming over me. *Am I hungry? Do I need to go outside?*

There was a yearning I couldn't explain. I sniffed the Asteria stone deeper, trying to understand what I felt.

"Think it would make a pretty collar?" Morgana said, chuckling to herself. "I wonder if you could make it work."

"What's that?" Merlin mumbled softly at the other end of the room.

My nostrils flared, and I whined. I wanted *something* very badly.

Morgana raised the silver chain and spread it between her hands. She let the glowing stone hang low beneath, and I felt my nostrils widen. Hairs stood up all over my body. She passed the chain over my snout, and sparks of light buzzed between my ears.

My mane glowed bright as the stone slid beneath my chin. "Very pretty," Morgana cooed, and her words were clear to me in a way I'd never felt before. The sounds were the same, the tone of voice not out of place, but something else came with them.

"This makes me feel strange," I said. My tongue felt tight, and air moved through my throat in an unfamiliar way.

Morgana's eyes bulged.

"Something's off about this stone, I think," I said in an odd voice. "Does the room seem brighter to you? Or no, not brighter. But something about it makes more sense!"

"Master Merlin!" Morgana cried, backing away from me—her hands outstretched.

"What is it?"

"I feel funny!" I said to Merlin, wagging my tail from side to side.

"Oh no!" he shouted, dropping a bottle of bubbling oil. My master ran toward me like my mane was on fire. He crashed into me, and I nearly fell off the table. His bony hands grasped around my neck.

"Be careful!" I said, but then my tongue thickened in my jaws. "Woof! Woof!"

The Asteria was off my neck.

"Master Merlin, he spoke!" Morgana said, her hands shaking and her face pale white.

"What were you thinking?" Merlin turned to her, clasping the chain.

"He spoke!" she said, her hands against her cheeks. "How did that happen?"

"I've heard stories," Merlin said, out of breath. "Animals finding them in the wild." He blinked hard and pressed a hand to his brow.

"It made him speak, Master," Morgana jabbered wildly. "He spoke to me just like a person."

Both stared at me, wide-eyed and amazed.

I glanced between them, racking my brain. *Speak!* I thought. *I've heard that word before.* Merlin had been saying it recently. It was some trick he wanted me to perform. He'd close his fingers and thumb and then . . . "Speak!" he'd say, and open his hand.

I hadn't known what he wanted before, but now I understood. And by the looks on their faces, I'd wowed them!

I readied myself to Speak! again. But all I could manage was "Woof!" Something wasn't quite the same. Still, Merlin and Morgana stared at me in silent awe.

Speak! was fun!

3

A Trick That's Not a Trick

THE FLUFFY BUNNY WAS TEARING ACROSS THE HILL AND I WAS nipping at the back of its heels. *I'm gonna get you, fluffy bunny!*

"Nosewise! Nosewise!" A loud whispering voice broke through the bright sky of my dream, and I found myself in a dark room surrounded by wrinkled blankets. My lips were wet with drool, and I licked them off, blinking and yawning.

"Nosewise!" The whispering came again. My eyes were bleary, and fuzzy shapes were hovering in the dark door frame. The shadows sorted themselves into a Morgana.

"Come, boy! Come here!" She was talking quietly and waving. I looked over my shoulder and saw Merlin fast asleep at the head of the bed. His stocking cap was pulled over his eyes, but his long eyebrow hairs poked out by his nose. His mouth was wide open, and he was snoring something awful.

"Nosewise, come!" Morgana's voice was getting higher-pitched, and she was flicking her fingers toward her like little paddles. My tail wagged wildly. I was happy Morgana had come to visit me.

I pushed off the bed and down to the floor. Then I shook my whole body and made a "woof!"

"Mmmm, Nosewise . . . be quiet," Merlin murmured, pulling his stocking cap farther over his face. Morgana tensed and put a finger to her lips. She ushered me out of the room by my behind, and I scurried into the den.

"Let's go outside," she whispered, opening the front door and waving for me to go through. I took a quick measurement of my bladder and realized I didn't have any business worth doing, but I walked outside anyway. I could always sniff around the garden.

As soon as I was out of the house, Morgana closed the door behind us and grabbed me by the scruff of my neck. I struggled against her for a moment—there were some very interesting chipmunk droppings by the cabbages—but she was stronger.

We marched out to the grassy field that surrounded Merlin's house in the woods. She told me to Sit! and I did so, being the sort of dog who likes performing the tricks that he knows. She sat down too.

"Nosewise," she said, settling to her knees, "I've brought this for you."

From out of her cloak she pulled the silver chain and

glowing stone. *The Asteria!* I thought, remembering the events of the day.

I'd finally mastered Speak!, and Morgana and Merlin had been very impressed. But instead of praising me, Merlin had ordered me out of the study at once. They hadn't let me back in, no matter how much I whined and begged. Then, at dinner, they'd spent the whole meal whispering in voices too low for me to hear. Very frustrating.

Morgana took a deep breath and spread the silver chain open with her fingers. She passed the loop over my snout until it rested in my mane. I felt my fur stand up again, and that wonderful buzz of light returned between my ears.

"I love this thing you've got," I said to Morgana. Her eyes grew wide, and her jaw went slack. "It makes me feel so happy, like I can do anything!"

"Nosewise, you're speaking," Morgana said in wonder.

"I know!" I said. "Now I've got a bunch! Sit! Shake! Lie down! And Speak!" My tail wagged so wildly that I had to stand up and let my whole backside waggle with it. "Merlin said something about Roll over! but I couldn't understand. Is it like this?" I tucked my head between my front legs and jumped.

"Nosewise, it's not a trick!" Morgana said, pulling my head up by my ears. "You're really talking to me!"

"It is too a trick," I said angrily. "Don't get jealous. You know tricks too."

"Nosewise, listen to me," Morgana said, putting her hands under my chin. "This is *magic*! Incredible magic! Something I've never seen or heard about. Merlin acts like he knows what's going on, but he doesn't have a clue. He's scared of it! No one's ever heard of a talking dog!"

I cocked my head at that one.

"So . . . ," I said, puzzling it out. "It's a trick no dog's ever learned? That should make Merlin happy!"

Morgana laughed, then covered her hand with her mouth. "Your mind," she said, giggling. "It's fantastic. The Asteria's brought what's in your head out into the world, just like it's supposed to do."

I didn't understand what she meant, but my tail wagged anyway. It *sounded* impressive.

A light filled the living room window. Morgana and I glanced through the smudgy glass and spotted Merlin in his nightcap. He was wandering the house with a lit candle.

"Oh, he's looking for us," I said, turning toward him excitedly. Just as quick, Morgana grabbed the silver chain and whipped it off my head. The buzzing light dimmed between my ears but didn't go completely out. "Woof! Woof!" I barked, trying to call Merlin over, but it was different. I'd forgotten how to Speak!

"Nosewise," Morgana said, whispering in my ear, "you can't tell Merlin about any of this. Well, of course you can't—not without the Asteria. But if you understand me now, just act normal. Merlin's forbidden me, but this is too important not to explore."

"Morgana? Nosewise?" Merlin croaked as he opened the door. His candle dripped hot wax onto his fingers, and he fiddled with it, cursing a bit. I found that he was much easier to understand than before.

"Nosewise was barking at the door," Morgana said. "I let him out to do his business, but now he's done. Come, Nosewise." Morgana flicked her head toward the house, and her black hair bounced against her shoulders. An all-around good feeling warmed me. My master, my pack mate, and a nice warm house to go to. All this and the promise of even greater tricks loomed, like fluffy bunnies, on the horizon.

I couldn't wait to catch them.

4

What Merlin Doesn't Know

THE NEXT DAY, MORGANA TOOK ME ON A LONG WALK IN THE woods around our home. We crossed the grassy clearing, and Morgana opened up the Wall of Trees, which kept us separated from the forest. Once we were past, she closed the Wall of Trees again to make sure Merlin didn't hear or see what we did.

"Here's what Merlin thinks we're looking for today," Morgana said, and held out some dried bramble leaf, a rotted mushroom, and a spindly tuber, things that were running low on the shelves in the study. "Find a basketful and we can start!"

I barked at that and raced through the woods. I loved tracking the scents Morgana gave me and leading her to spots where she'd find more of the same. As soon as we found enough of each, she patted my head and took me to a special spot in the woods that she'd prepared. It was a little ravine with a stream running through it and three fallen oaks that made a sort of a roof. Morgana called it the Outdoor Study.

She'd brought cauldrons there and scraps of paper weighted down with stones. I saw a tidy pile of bones in one corner, and several clay jars sat beside an ashy fire pit.

In the center of it all was a hollowed-out tree stump filled with glassy water. The stump had a smell so interesting I was tempted to dip my nose in it, but Morgana shooed me away when I got close.

Then she commanded Sit!, put the Asteria round my neck, and asked me *questions*.

"Here, I have ten cards," she said. "I painted a color on each. Which are the same and which are different?"

I squinted at the tiny pieces of paper she'd lined up against a rock. I padded toward them to give a sniff—each smelled quite distinct.

"No sniffing allowed," Morgana said, holding up her hand. "Can you tell the difference with your eyes?"

My tail waggled slightly. "Those five are yellow," I said, tossing my head to the left. "And those other five are blue."

"Really?" Morgana said, looking surprised. "You see yellow and blue? But not any other colors? Not green here? Not orange?" she said, pointing to different cards.

I blinked at her, not knowing *what* she was talking about.

"You know, many people think dogs can't see color at all," she said, tapping her chin. "But from your answers, I'd guess you're only partially color-blind."

"Hey, I can see colors," I said. "I'm not blind!"

"Humans can see seven different colors, Nosewise. You're only seeing two."

My ears perked up. "Are you trying to fool me?" I asked, getting wise to Morgana's game. "Because I can see all the colors that there are . . . both of them!"

She had me pick up drops of flower essence from cauldrons of rainwater. "You can smell one part per ten million!" Morgana crowed. "That's amazing!"

"Can't we find something better to smell?" I asked, tired of picking out flowers. "Like deer cakes! Those have a lovely smell."

"You mean the droppings deer leave in the woods?" Morgana said flatly.

"Yes! That would make a good game. I could find them for you!"

"I don't want you to find 'deer cakes,' Nosewise. I'm testing the sensitivity of your nose."

"Well, why not test how long it takes me to find a skunk carcass? I think I smell one just upwind," I said, twitching my nose in the air. But Morgana made a sour face. She wasn't very open to *my* ideas.

Later she led me to a trail she'd walked earlier that day and asked if I could tell in which direction she'd gone.

"This way!" I pronounced, after a moment of snuffling.

"That's right," she said, sticking out her tongue. "Now, how did you know that?"

"Well, I can smell you on the ground. Your scent is all over."

"Tiny flakes of my hair and skin fall off me all the time," she said, getting to her knees. "But how could you know the *direction* I was walking? Couldn't I have laid this trail going either way?"

"The odor's faded going *that* way," I said. "Which means it's older."

"Yes, but it's only seconds older," she said, disbelieving. "Can you really sense the difference?"

"Of course! Can't you?"

"No," she said, laughing. "My nose is nothing compared to yours."

I felt sad for Morgana. No *wonder* she didn't like deer cakes.

*   *   *

Toward the end of the afternoon, she was blowing into a tiny whistle to see if I could hear the sound.

"Yes, of course I can hear it!" I shouted. "You're blowing in my ear!"

Morgana held the grass whistle to her chest. "I'm testing the range of your hearing!"

"Well, I think these tricks are terrible!" I said, stalking about the leaf litter. "Smell water? Look at paper? It makes Sit! seem exciting. Teach me the tricks *you* know how to do! Shooting lightning and fire! Disappearing things!"

"Nosewise," Morgana said, dropping down before me, "these aren't tricks I'm having you do. They're experiments. This is an opportunity for dogs and humans to understand one another."

"I want to shoot lightning! Teach me!"

"I've already told you: that's magic!" Morgana said sternly. "It's nothing to be fooled with!"

"Then don't fool me with it," I said, sitting and curling my tail around my paws. My ears pressed down against my head and my eyes went wide. "I see the way Merlin looks at you when you do those tricks"—Morgana opened her mouth to correct me—"that *magic*! I want to learn it too."

"Hmm." Morgana leaned down on her elbow and rubbed my ear. "You're already practicing magic, Nosewise. A kind I've never seen before."

"I am? Well, what is magic, then?" I said, waggling my tail.

Morgana glanced at the hollowed-out tree trunk filled with glassy water. She took a short breath and turned back to me. "I'll show you."

We tracked our way backward until we came to the Wall of Trees.

"Do you know what this is?" Morgana asked, placing her hand on an oak.

"Yes! Yes, I know!" I said. "That's the Wall of Trees." I jumped on my hind legs and wagged my tail.

"That's right," she said with a smile. "But *what* is it?"

I came down to my forepaws. "It's a wall," I hazarded, "of trees?"

"It's a magical barrier," Morgana corrected me. "A powerful enchantment grown out of Merlin's desire to protect what he holds dear. Watch."

She brushed her hand against an oak, and the ground beneath us began to shake. The Wall of Trees was made of a thousand huge oak trees all pressed so tightly together you couldn't peek between them. Their branches grasped each other in knots so complicated you couldn't tell where one started and another began. But the tree Morgana touched started to bend. Its branches unwound from its fellows, and the whole enormous oak leaned forward, making a slim opening into the clearing around Merlin's house.

"It's a door!" I said, thinking I'd found the answer.

Stupid door, I thought privately.

"It's not a door," Morgana said. "A door can be opened by any hand—"

"Not mine!" I said.

"You don't have hands. And don't interrupt," Morgana said. My ears pressed to the sides of my head. "The Wall of Trees is magic. An enchantment. For Merlin and for me, it opens at a touch. But not fire, nor lightning, nor a battering ram could break down these trees otherwise."

I glanced at the enormous circle of oaks that curved around our home in the woods. "Are all trees that way?" I'd relieved myself on so many trees throughout my life, it made me tremble to think they were so powerful.

"No," Morgana answered. "The Asteria you wear brings what's inside of you out. What Merlin wanted when he came to this out-of-the-way place was to be left alone. His will and Certainty are so strong that he grew a circle of enchanted trees to protect him."

"To protect him from what?"

"Strangers, of course," Morgana answered. "Do you know what to do if you meet a stranger? Let's say a stranger offering you food?"

"If they're offering you food," I said, thinking it out, "then that means they're good and you should trust them with your life!"

"No! Nosewise!" Morgana shouted. "That's the opposite of what you should do!"

I winced and dropped my tail between my legs.

"You don't know what's out there in the world," she said. "People are dangerous."

My ears were pressed against my head. "When I first met Merlin, he was a stranger offering me food," I said. "And trusting him was the best thing I ever did."

Morgana crouched and looked me in the eyes. "I know, boy. I'm sorry. What was your life like before Merlin found you?"

It felt somehow as if a stone had formed at the base of my stomach. My shoulders tensed and my tail went stiff.

"It's not a happy memory."

"Then forget it," Morgana said. "I try not to think of my life before Merlin found me. But look at us now," she said, standing up. "Wards of the most famous and powerful wizard in the world. Lucky is what you and I are."

I stood up at that, panting and wagging my tail.

"Give me the Asteria," she said, pulling the chain off my neck. "And let's head back to the house. See what the old man's cooking up."

"Woof! Woof!"

5

The Monster in the Leaves

Every day after that one, Morgana and I searched the woods for potion ingredients.

I'd find them fast, and we'd spend the rest of our time in the Outdoor Study. I learned lots of things there. For instance, at first I'd thought that Morgana and I were *both* pets. But as it turned out, only I was a pet, and she was what is called an *apprentice*. She was proud of that, but secretly I knew that being a pet was better, because it meant you got *petted*, which was really nice.

Another thing I learned was that Morgana was twelve years old. I nearly fell over when I heard that—Morgana was ancient! But she told me that though that might *seem* old to a dog, for a girl like her it was really quite young. I asked how old Merlin was, but she said I couldn't handle it.

One thing I didn't like was that Morgana refused to teach me how to *do* magic. She never let me try to shoot

lightning or fire out of the Asteria; she said it was dangerous. I didn't see what would be so bad about it; I never hurt
myself trying to Sit! or Shake!

But she did say it was all right to teach me *about* magic,
which was almost as fun, I suppose.

"There are two schools of magic," Morgana said on our fifth
day in the Outdoor Study. "Summer and Winter."

"Are they like the seasons?" I asked. "Summer magic
makes things hot and Winter magic chills them?"

"No, that's not quite right," Morgana said, sitting down
on a log. I walked toward her but got too close to the
hollowed-out tree trunk for her liking, and she ushered me
away. She never did let me get near that trunk—though I
really was entranced by it. The whole base was covered with
a stinky moss that seemed to pulsate like a heartbeat. It was
all I could do to stop myself from rubbing against it.

"It is easier, of course, to chill with Winter and heat with
Summer," Morgana said, pulling me close. "But both can
really accomplish either."

"Then I think they named them wrong. They should
have named them *sort of* Winter and *sort of* Summer."

Morgana laughed. "And who are *they* supposed to be?"
she asked with a smile.

"I don't know," I answered. "Whoever named magic."

Morgana grew quiet and glanced at the trunk herself.

What was *that thing?*

"Summer magic strikes fast and strong," she said, dropping into a low, gruff voice. "Winter magic lasts a lifetime long."

My tail wagged. "That's Merlin!"

"It's a rhyme he taught me when I first started," said Morgana. She passed her hand over my head and rubbed my neck. "The schools of magic are vast and mysterious, but that rhyme can help. Summer magic is cast easily, but its power fades. Winter magic is harder to do, but it's more lasting and"—she snuck another peek at the trunk and whispered—"some say more powerful."

"Which do you do?" I asked.

"Summer," Morgana said, and smiled bashfully. She tucked her black hair behind an ear. "Merlin's a master of both—he learned Winter magic from the best. But he says Summer's easier for beginners."

"So how *do* you make things hot and cold?" I asked, wagging my tail and stretching my neck.

"That's *elemental* magic, Nosewise; I've told you already."

"Right, I know!" I said, straightening up. "Elemental is fire, ice, and force. Illusion is disappearing, spirits, and hammers."

"*Glamours,* Nosewise. Not hammers," Morgana said. "What's a glamour do?"

"It's a . . . thing that . . ." I racked my brain for what Morgana had said.

"A glamour makes something appear that isn't there, or look like something it's not." She tapped her finger against my snout. "Why can you remember where you buried a bone last month, but not something I said yesterday?"

"Because a bone is real," I said, standing up. "It's not just words. You never let me see the magic or try it. You act like it's just a story."

"Nosewise," Morgana said, dropping her chin, "I let you do much more than Merlin ever would."

"Which is nothing, I know. But it feels like you're teasing me."

"I'm *teaching* you," Morgana said, folding her hands in her lap. "As much as I think is safe."

"What's a Certainty?" I asked, feeling my heart beat faster in my chest. "I've heard you and Merlin talk about it."

"I can't tell you that."

"Why not?"

"Because I don't know what you could do with it."

"Well, how would you ever know?" I said, agitated. "All day I'm stuck in the house. And even out here you close doors on me. It's not fair!"

"Nosewise, relax."

"You ask me questions all the time!" I shouted. "Answer the ones that *I* want to know! What's a Certainty? How do I explode the front door off Merlin's house so I can pee when I want? And why can't I go near that tree trunk?"

I pointed toward the water-filled trunk that sat at the center of the Outdoor Study and felt the urge to take a drink.

"Nosewise, don't go near that."

I glanced back at her and walked toward it.

"I'm serious—stay back!" Morgana said, standing up. She snapped her fingers and glowered at me.

She's not the master, I thought. *She's only a pet like me. Or worse than a pet—an apprentice!*

I bounded forward across the crunchy leaves and jumped against the thick rim of the tree trunk. In the glassy waters I saw my face reflected and noticed that the Asteria around my neck was glowing brightly.

"Get the Asteria away from there!" Morgana cried.

"But why?" I whined. "Nothing bad happened."

"WHO CALLS ME?" A low and powerful voice echoed across the forest floor.

The hairs stood up on my head. The Asteria was spinning now, and droplets of water from the trunk flowed upward into the air.

"Nosewise, down! Down, boy!"

"Sorry!" I said, dropping from the trunk and backing away. A strong wind pressed against me, and leaves and twigs swirled through the air. They mixed into a tower of water gushing up from the trunk, and the voice rumbled again.

"WHO CALLS ME?"

"What's happening?" I shouted.

"It's his fountain—it's his glade. You called him!"

"Who?" I asked. Leaves, pine needles, and dirt spun like a tornado and resolved into the shape of a man.

"My father. Get out of here, quick!" Morgana screamed at me.

I ran.

6

The Summoning Stump

"NOSEWISE!"

A small voice bounced through the trees.

I was hunkered down in a faraway safe-spot, pinched between two huge tree roots.

"Nosewise!" the voice called again.

"Morgana?" I said, raising my head. "I'm here!"

"I can't see you!" Morgana shouted, her voice louder.

I emerged from my safe-spot and cautiously tracked through the woods. I spotted her struggling up a hill of muddy grass. She was holding branches for support. "Morgana, I'm here!"

"Oh, Nosewise!" she said, dropping down to a muddy patch and running over. "The most wonderful thing has happened."

"What?" I said, walking up to her. She embraced me warmly. Her hair was stuck with leaves and twigs, and her face smelled like fire.

She grasped my cheeks with the flats of her hands and pressed her nose to mine. "Come with me."

We found the Outdoor Study in awful shape. The cauldrons were all turned over, the logs Morgana used as seats were singed, and the mossy tree trunk was gone.

The ground it had sat on was black and blasted out— only an ashy pit remained.

"What happened there?" I asked, my tail gone stiff.

"He said he didn't need it anymore," Morgana answered with a sly smile.

"Who said? Morgana, what's going on? That was scary!"

"Sorry, Nosewise. I didn't want you frightened."

"Well, I am!" I answered truthfully. "A whole lot of dirt and leaves turned into a monster!"

Morgana giggled. "Not a monster, Nosewise." She plopped down on the scorched earth and gestured for me to sit across from her. "Remember how you said that before Merlin found you, your life was bad?"

"Yeah," I answered.

"Mine was too. My mother died when I was little, and I never knew my father—had no family to speak of. Until I was nine, I lived on the streets in Chester, which is where I think you came from."

My ears sank.

"I begged for food and slept where I could. Until a kind old man named Merlin found me. He said I had a Knack for magic, though I didn't know what that was. Then he brought me here."

"You trusted a stranger too."

"I did—and it was the best thing that ever happened to me." Morgana flashed her eyes, and a broad smile spread across her face. "Until my father came."

"Your father?"

"That was him just now."

I blinked and cocked my head. "The dirt and leaves are your father?"

Morgana put her hand to her chest and laughed. "No, Nosewise," she said, wiping away a tear. "He's far away. That's just how he speaks to me. When you brought the Asteria close to the Summoning Stump, it called him."

I looked at Morgana for a long moment.

"I don't understand."

She laughed again. "I didn't think you would. But he's coming here tonight. You can meet him."

"Really? Coming here?"

"Yes, and in the flesh this time," Morgana said. She balled her hands into excited fists. "So far, I've only seen him as leaves and wind!"

"That's . . . wonderful," I said. I was happy for Morgana, but I wasn't sure about a man made of leaves.

"It's not so odd when you know him. He's quite power-ful, very adept." Morgana pressed her fingers to her lips and squealed. "And he's got a castle! Can you imagine that?"

"Not really. What's a castle?"

"Like a house made of stones, but very, very large."

"Does Merlin know about this?" I asked, trying to hide my discomfort.

"What? No, of course not! Why do you think I come here?" She threw her hands at the wreckage of the Outdoor Study. "So Father can visit me when I need him and teach me things Merlin never would."

"You've been doing this a long time?"

"Since this winter, when I first found that old Summon-ing Stump."

"Summoning Stump?"

"It's an enchantment that wizards use to talk to others in faraway places. Merlin must have made it a long time ago, because it was covered with leaves and dirt. But when I walked by with my Asteria, it called out to me."

"Like it did just now," I asked, slightly wide-eyed.

Morgana laughed. "At first I thought I'd seen a ghost. But then he spoke to me and told me who he was: my father, who'd been looking for me everywhere!"

I wondered if someday my father might visit me as a bunch of leaves. I didn't know it worked like that. I was learning *a lot* in the woods.

"Merlin is a great wizard, the best in the world, but *conservative*," Morgana said, gathering up burned papers and tossing them in the stream. "Always with the same old phrase: 'Magic is for those with the wisdom to wield it!'"

"I've heard him say that!"

"You know, Merlin would say *you* don't have the wisdom to wield magic. He wouldn't have even let you sit with us inside the study. I had to suggest it."

"I've been good in the study!"

"Yes, you have. So Merlin's not always right, is he?" Morgana asked, arching her eyebrow.

"I—I suppose sometimes he's wrong," I answered hesitantly. It went against everything I felt as a dog to speak badly of my master.

"Sometimes others have to act for his own good. And that's why we *can't let him know about this,* all right?" Morgana looked up at the sky. "It's getting dark, and he'll worry."

As we trudged back through the dimming woods, Morgana giggled to herself. "Father has such a wonderful quest for Merlin," she said, bursting with excitement. "He wants me to make the introduction."

She was positively skipping. It made me excited too.

We reached the Wall of Trees and Morgana turned to me with a jerk. "Tonight!" she said, spreading her hands to the air. "Father will arrive in the forest. I'll creep from bed and sneak out of the house." She acted each step, dancing and leaping.

"I'll run across the meadow," she said. "Come to the Wall of Trees—"

"And open it up?" I said, lifting my forepaws against an oak.

The roots shook beneath my feet. Morgana's eyes went wide and looked down.

The branches of the oak unknotted themselves from their fellows. The whole tree creaked and groaned, bending forward.

"It's opening," I said, looking at the tree. My tail wagged wildly. "I'm opening the Wall of Trees!" I shouted. "I'm opening it! I'm doing magic!"

"You are!" Morgana said. "How?"

The enormous tree trunk leaned away from me with a moan, and revealed, behind it, a robed man with a long white beard. He took his hand off the oak and stared at us.

7

Even Magic Has Rules

"Nosewise, take that off!" Merlin said, his eyes popping.

I leapt back in shock. He pointed at me.

"Drop it, now."

"I'm sorry," I answered, glancing at Morgana. "I—I just wanted to learn the tricks."

Merlin put one hand on the leaning tree and crossed to me. I backed away, not wanting to lose my voice.

"Don't be mad at Morgana. It's my fault, not hers."

"Drop the stone!" Merlin commanded, slapping his palms together. I lowered my head, and the silver chain slid down my neck. The Asteria landed in leaves and pine needles.

Merlin bent down to pick it up. I tried to apologize again, but my voice was gone.

Merlin gently took hold of my chin. "Are you all right, my boy?"

"He's fine," Morgana answered for me. "I was watching him."

"*This* is looking for potion ingredients?" Merlin said with a sharp tongue. "You lied to me."

"We did look for them. We were just . . . doing this, too."

"You put him in danger. I thought you cared for Nosewise."

"It was *safe*," Morgana said in a pleading voice. "I know it was."

"You are an apprentice. You don't know what's safe and what isn't. Magic is for those—"

"With the wisdom to wield it. Yes, I've heard."

"All right," Merlin said, straightening himself. He looked at Morgana and me, anger and guilt flashing across his face. "We're going home."

The three of us walked through the clearing in silence. Merlin and Morgana didn't want to talk. I didn't have a choice.

When we got back to the house, Merlin walked into the study. He unlocked a high cabinet and placed Morgana's Asteria inside.

"That's my Asteria," she said.

"It isn't yours," Merlin said, sighing. He locked the cabinet and walked back into the living room. "Letting Nosewise into the study was my mistake." Merlin's eyes watered, and his lips pressed together. "And everything after, too. I'm your teacher, so what you do is my responsibility."

"It wasn't so bad," Morgana said. Her fists were balled so tight her knuckles went white. "All I did was let him play a little."

"Would you let a dog play with a crossbow?" Merlin said, his tone sad and firm. I shrank in the corner of the room. "That Asteria can command a lightning bolt, a fireball, a blast of wind."

"He's not simple. He's very smart."

"And so are you. You should know better—"

"Don't lecture me!" Morgana snapped. "There's more to magic than *you* know."

"Aye, there is. I know enough of my ignorance to fear magic and respect it."

"Well, I'm not afraid," Morgana said, sticking out her chin.

Merlin narrowed his eyes. "This isn't you."

Morgana looked away uncomfortably. I could hear her swallow, and she let her shoulders relax. "I'm sorry," she said, calming herself. "I won't do it again."

"I thank you for that."

"Now," Morgana said, extending her hand, "may I *please* have my Asteria back?"

"You may use it in our lessons," Merlin answered. "Under my supervision."

46

Morgana stared at him silently.

"Morgana," Merlin said gently, "I'm not punishing you. I'm only trying to help."

She shook her head and blinked tears from her eyes. "You're a good man, Merlin," she said with a wavering voice. "But you have a closed mind. Someone needs to open it for you." Morgana marched into her bedroom and swiftly shut the door.

Slam! The noise made me jump, and I skittered under the kitchen table.

Merlin looked at me.

"Nosewise, I'm sorry. I'm sorry," he murmured. "Here, have a—have a treat." Merlin opened a jar where he kept old bones. I peeked out from under the table.

"Take it," he said, offering a bone. "No tricks required."

I smelled the marrow and snatched it. For a moment my mind was filled with the task of chewing the bone—focused on the feel and the flavor.

Merlin was on the floor beside me, stroking my head.

"I'm not sure how much you still understand," he said. I stopped chewing and looked up, which seemed to surprise him. "Maybe a lot."

He nodded at the bone, and I went back to chewing it.

"When I took you from that place, I wanted to give you a life where you wouldn't worry or want for anything. But to keep you safe, I confine you. To preserve your health, I control your food. And I've given you very little choice in all of this."

I dropped the bone and whined.

"I feel guilty about it. But I don't know a better way to take care of you. The world is a dangerous place, and I can only do so much to protect you."

I raised my head to him and he rubbed my cheek.

"You clearly have a Knack," Merlin said, and that perked my ears. "But magic is like a powerful river. A skilled boatman sails swiftly. But someone without the ability to understand . . . they can drown."

I looked over at the cabinet that held the Asteria and felt my whiskers twitch. I'd upset Merlin and gotten Morgana into trouble. I'd wanted to impress him and maybe learn how to open the door. But it had all gone horribly wrong.

"Magic," Merlin said, standing to shut the door to the study, "is *not* for everyone." He smiled kindly and sat next to me again.

I knew what he'd really meant to say.

Magic wasn't for *me*.

8

A Bump in the Night

THE FLUFFY BUNNY WAS CHASING ME NOW. IT HAD LONG TEETH and enormous paws. *Get away from me!* I shouted. Its claws clattered like metal swords—

I woke up at the foot of Merlin's bed.

Something wasn't right.

I perked my ears to the night and heard groaning wood. Branches were bending and snapping.

I glanced back at Merlin. He was never vigilant.

I jumped off the foot of the bed and squeezed my way through the bedroom door. The fire in the hearth was dead and dark. The house felt entirely too still. I turned to my right and saw that Morgana's bedroom door was open.

Her father was coming that night, I remembered. Was she opening the Wall of Trees?

I walked over the thick, woven rug and leapt up on the stuffed chair that sat by the window. I put my forepaws on the sill and peered through the glass.

The moon sat low in the sky and cast a misty light over the clearing that surrounded our house. My breath was fogging the glass.

Something perked my ears. A man was speaking. Several men.

All of a sudden, it seemed very wrong that Morgana's father should appear as a ghostly figure of leaves and then visit in the dead of night.

I barked and jumped down, ran into Merlin's room, and leapt on the bed.

"Oh!" he called out, waking up. I stood over his face, whining and crying.

"Nosewise!" he said, pushing me away. I glanced toward the living room. Merlin was slow to stir.

I nudged him with the wet of my nose.

"What's the matter?" Merlin asked, lifting his nightcap.

I barked.

"Something bad?"

Merlin caught my tone. His eyebrows twitched, and he pushed the covers off. He was slow to grab his robe from the hook, and I barked again.

"All right," he said. "I'm going!" He slipped it over his shoulders and ambled into the den. I ran ahead of him and jumped on the chair, pressing my nose to the glass.

"You're fogging it up," Merlin said, wiping the window with his sleeve. He peered into the night.

"The Wall of Trees is open . . . ," Merlin said, grabbing the back of the chair. "Soldiers coming through," he whispered. "Lord Destrian!"

I pushed to see for myself, but my vision was blurry and I could see only shadows.

"Morgana," Merlin called, rushing to her room, "wake up! We're under attack!" He tore the cold covers off her bed. "Where is she?"

I barked.

"We'll fight them off," Merlin said, rubbing his chest. "Then we'll find Morgana. They're just men with swords. Good boy, Nosewise!" He ran off toward the study and I followed.

Did Morgana let those soldiers in?

Merlin unlocked the high cabinet, where the most dangerous potions were kept. He hastily grabbed bottles, which bubbled and glowed when he touched them. In his rush he knocked Morgana's Asteria off the shelf, and it fell to the floor at my feet. It sparked when it hit the stones, and I felt a tiny tingle in my head. Merlin took no notice.

He stuffed the vials into his pockets and charged from the study, holding his staff. I ran, barking, at his heels. Merlin opened the big wood front door and blocked me with his leg. "Nosewise, I have to go. Stay here," he commanded.

He slipped out and slammed the door shut behind him.

I looked up at the heavy door. Merlin was on the other

side. I jumped and put my nose on the handle, jiggling it desperately.

A door was a door, and doors didn't open for me.

I scrambled back to the big stuffed chair, dislodging the rug beneath my feet. I spotted Merlin through the window.

Now I could see soldiers. The moonlight reflected in their shiny armor.

Maybe twenty surrounded Merlin. Some held clubs and others had nets. I barked wildly, trying to get his attention. *Why* won't *he let me come and fight?* His long gray robe flowed from the top of his head to the ground. In his right hand he held the knotty staff, and his Asteria brightened.

Merlin shouted something and thrust his staff at the soldiers. It was a shock spell; I could see the air ripple ahead of him and the armored men knocked onto their backs.

The Asteria glowed as bright as the moon and cast the soldiers in cold blue light. Three men charged him from the right. I barked and he spun, casting a spike of ice. The blast exploded at their feet, and the men screamed. Ice crystals froze them to the earth, and they hacked at them with their clubs.

Merlin unplugged a blue bottle and flames leapt from it. He blew across the top of the glass, and a wide arc of fire spread before him. The soldiers stumbled away, afraid of getting burned. I barked in triumph. Merlin was winning.

"Be gone!" I heard him yell. He threw the vial into the grass, and it erupted in a towering inferno. Behind the wall of fire I watched Merlin uncork another vial and shake its contents into the air. White strands of mist fell to the ground. As the column of fire lessened, the strands took the shape of ghostly wolves, which charged at the moonlit soldiers.

They were just illusions, I could tell, but the invaders were afraid of them. The ghosts snapped and foamed at their mouths, herding the soldiers into a tight group.

"Leave my lands!" Merlin shouted. He stamped his staff again, and a bolt of lightning toasted the grass beneath the soldiers' feet.

The armored men were panicking. They fumbled in all directions and tripped over each other. The fallen ones scrambled up, and the standing ones turned to run.

"Steady!" A booming voice echoed over the clearing. "Hold and ready!"

The horde of soldiers cleared an aisle, and a bright, gleaming man walked between them.

His armor caught the light from the moon and reflected it back brighter. Where the other men had shadowy faces and dingy outfits, this new soldier was all luster, bronze plate laced with silver. His face was square and strong, framed by a helmet that sprouted two large, golden wings above the ears. The sword in his hand reflected Merlin's image like a mirror. He was Lord Destrian.

Wrapped around his sword were three glowing strands

of light. They unraveled and slithered through the air like worms. They spiraled up and then dove toward Merlin's wolves. The ghostly wolves growled and snapped their jaws, but the strands shot straight through them. As they passed, they sucked the wolves into nothingness, like smoke disappearing up a chimney.

Then the worms shivered and grew bigger.

The soldiers started organizing themselves.

I saw Merlin widen his stance and lift his staff. He held it for a moment while the Asteria glowed. Then he leveled it at Lord Destrian and unleashed a fireball as big as a bushel of hay.

It hurtled through the smoking air, but the worms whipped around and dove into the fire like it was an enormous apple. In a moment it was extinguished, and the worms grew larger in the smoke.

Lord Destrian stepped away from the men. He stomped toward Merlin and sheathed his sword.

Merlin sent a blast of ice at him. A worm lashed out and gulped it down like a fly. Merlin sent another wide wave of shock, but two worms flew in front and caught the spell. They glowed and grew bigger. They were eating his magic.

The wiggling things darted into Merlin's Asteria and fastened themselves there like parasites. The stone went dark and the worms glowed.

Merlin tried to protect himself with his staff, but Lord Destrian knocked it away. He brought an armored fist down on Merlin's head.

I launched myself at the window, barking madly. *I have to help him!*

I jumped off the back of the chair and ran to the study. Morgana's Asteria was there, jumbled on the floor. I bit the silver chain with my teeth and shook my head wildly, flinging the stone above my head. I let go and, miraculously, the chain slipped around my neck.

A light buzzed between my ears. The tingly magic tickled my nose.

And I ran to the door of our house.

"Open! Open!" I commanded, finding my voice. I jumped against the heavy door. My eyes strained against the wood. *Fire, lightning, shock! Anything!*

The Asteria was magic—but how did it work?

"Open!" I begged. I put my snout to the handle and furiously bit. "Open! Open!"

Stupid door! I charged back to the stuffed chair and looked through the window.

Lord Destrian had Merlin's limp body slung over his shoulder. I looked closely at Merlin's back. It rose and fell. He was breathing and alive.

"Let him go!" I shouted at the window. "Don't hurt him!"

Lord Destrian was conferring with some soldiers. Something about his face looked strange. He paid me no attention.

"Let him go!" I shouted again, and slammed into the glass with my snout. I launched myself against it but couldn't break through. "Please!" I pleaded. My voice was a high-pitched squeal. "Don't take him!"

The other soldiers were a blur in the background. Lord Destrian yanked the glowing worms off Merlin's Asteria. They'd grown big as gardener snakes.

A soldier wandering near the house bent down and reached into the grass. He came up again with a gleaming glass vial. He squinted and uncorked the stop with his thumb. Air hit the elixir, and fire spewed out like a torch.

The man flinched and threw the potion in the air. I barked at him furiously.

The roof above me burst into flame.

9

Trapped in the House

THE STUDY DOOR WAS OPEN, AND I SAW FIERY ROOF THATCH falling on the floor. Merlin's potion made it burn bright and hot.

I heard a pop. Then another. Glass bottles were breaking apart in the heat.

The air thickened with smells. I recognized ingredients Merlin and Morgana had ground up and boiled down into potions. One was for healing cuts, they'd said—twenty-three ingredients. Another was for sleep—fifteen. A third they had put on my paws when I stepped in the itchy plant that grew by the Wall of Trees—five ingredients.

They were potions kept on the bottom shelves—the ones Merlin said were safe.

I peeked into the study and saw the flames lick higher and higher. The glass vials on the top shelves bubbled in the heat.

I skittered across the floor of the den, dove under the

kitchen table, and pressed up against the wall—as far away from the study as I could get.

Another glass broke.

The sound of thunder reverberated throughout the house.

A blast of energy erupted behind me and smashed *all the bottles of potion* Merlin had stored in the cabinets lining the wall. I smelled ingredients from fire, wind, lightning, and ice potions; they blasted their violence through the study doorway. I was protected from the force by the heavy stone wall, but thick, flaming goop splattered into the den.

The woven rug that I'd lain on a thousand times ignited and blackened, curling in on itself. The bone I'd been chewing on the floor burst as the marrow boiled inside it. The big stuffed chair smoked, and Merlin's teakettle glowed with heat.

Bad smells rushed up my nose with the smoke. There was a magic thunderstorm in the study, and blasts of lightning shot across the living room and went up the chimney. Swirling gray clouds floated out, raining frozen hail, which boiled in midair above the flames.

Ghostly eagles and foxes, and one tangle-haired demon, scurried from the study. *Just illusions,* I tried to tell myself, but I cowered as they danced through the fire. A wispy demon appeared under the kitchen table and pulled his cheeks apart with his fingers. "Bleegh!"

The illusions, I knew, couldn't hurt me, but the heat and lightning were real. I panted hard, and my mouth burned from smoke. My head ached like there was a knife in my skull, and I crawled from under the table, keeping my side to the stone wall, which was growing very warm.

I came up against the heavy front door. It was shut. There was smoke everywhere. My chin fell to the stones.

Fix what you want in your Mind's Eye, Merlin had said. I tried to imagine a freezing wind. What would that look like?

My Mind's Eye was bleary. The roar of the flames filled my ears, and every breath burned my chest.

I was crumpled in a heap, the heat burying all thoughts. My body was relaxing. I was slipping into darkness.

I twitched. My chest expanded, and I took one last sniff through my nostrils.

I caught a scent, and a part of me I'd never even thought to name lit up like a bonfire:

My Mind's *Nose.*

Through the crack underneath the door I smelled tender summer grass.

It filled me with a thought. One last thought. One powerful, magical thought:

I want to go outside.

Crash! My head slumped forward an inch. Wood slammed against stone. Fresh air filled my nostrils.

Grasping, gulping, I dragged myself through the now-open door frame. The Asteria hung in my mane. It was spinning and glowing intensely. The door of our house was wide open and breaking off the hinges.

The door was a door, after all. But I'd opened it.

I'd nearly blown it apart.

"*Stupid door,*" I whispered, crawling into the grass.

My eyes scanned for Merlin, but they were caked with gunk. My head was cloudy. There were sounds somewhere. In front of me or behind? Man or magic?

My head drooped into the grass. Soft. Fragrant. My breathing slowed. Everything did.

And then there was darkness. And silence.

But I was alive.

10

The Bad Master

THERE WAS A TIME BEFORE I KNEW ANYTHING ABOUT MERLIN OR magic or the wonders of the world. I was born in a dark place with a litter of puppies, but I can't remember much about them. For most dogs, your family is your master. And at the start of my life, I had a bad one.

The dark place was beneath the porch of a little house, and the man who owned it was my first master.

He chased my mother off as soon as he found us. Then, one by one, other masters came and took my brothers and sisters. None picked me.

The bad master wanted me to do a trick. He'd put leather sleeves over his arms and hit me in the face. "Attack!" he'd shout.

Then he'd hit me harder and yell, "Attack! Attack!"

It made me cower. I didn't like this trick.

The bad master didn't want me. When winter came, he

tied me to a tree by the road. He set out a bowl of water and some scraps. But he didn't come back.

I was tied to that tree for weeks. I ate all the snow that I could reach. People rode by in wagons and glared at me.

I was hungry and thirsty. The world looked cold and mean.

One day, when I was so weak that I could barely stand, an old man came walking by alongside a mule. His shawl covered his face, and he held a long staff that had a strange smell coming off the handle.

"Hello," he said, bending down and offering his hand.

I lifted my chin and sniffed him.

"Did someone leave you here?" he asked. His eyes were soft and kind. Somewhere deep in his robes . . . I smelled bacon.

"Oh hoo hoo!" he laughed when I nosed around his armpit. "You must be very hungry." He plunged his hand into a pocket and pulled out a cloth bundle. The greasy fabric opened and revealed thick hunks of smoked pork.

"Here you are," he said, offering me a piece. I was slow to eat but very appreciative. My tail wagged for the first time in days. "Pace yourself," he said, handing me another. "You have a very good nose. . . . That might make a fitting name."

He laid the handle of his staff on the rope that bound me to the tree. I heard a sizzle and the leash went slack.

"Nosewise," he said, scratching my head. "I think I'll call you that. And you, of course, can call me Merlin."

I woke up in the ashy grass and blinked my eyes. It was morning.

Over my shoulder I saw that the house was completely burned out. No more food bowl, no more warm carpet, no more Merlin to come home to.

I stood and sniffed the ground. The soldiers' scents were all there. I found that Lord Destrian smelled different from the others—there was something odd about him. Merlin was mixed in with the rest, and I followed the trail across the grassy field.

The Wall of Trees was open, and I found Morgana's scent with the soldiers' and some horses'.

Did Morgana know what would happen when she opened the wall? And Lord Destrian, is he her father who appeared in the leaves?

I followed them as the trail snaked between the trees. A party of humans and horses was easy to track. Besides their scents there were snapped twigs and branches and muddy hoofprints all along the forest floor.

I thought back to the joy I'd found at Merlin's house. I'd been petted, fed, loved, and protected. Was that all gone?

Merlin saved me once, I thought, following the scents into the woods.

Now it was my turn to save him.

PART II

11

So That's a Castle

THE SOLDIERS' SCENTS WEAVED THROUGH THE FOREST AND ONTO a dusty road. I followed them past pretty farms and grazing herds of sheep. I tracked them all day, never lifting my nose from the trail. The sun set and it got dark, but I kept tracking. After a long night of sniffing blind, the sun rose again, and I saw I was approaching a slow river. I was so thirsty I had to stop and take a drink.

As I lapped up the water, a hint of leather lodged in my nostrils. I popped up to sniff it and noticed a bright white shape off in the middle distance. The dawn sun reflected against it and made me squint.

The scent trail drew me nearer, and the great white shape grew larger and more detailed. Soon I could see it was built like an enormous house—giant, as big as the biggest hill I'd ever seen—and made of white stones.

Didn't Morgana call that a castle? She said her father had a castle.

Most of it was hidden behind a high wall. But I saw balconies and oval windows carved into the stones. A tall tower grew up from the middle and sprouted statues and flags like a branching tree.

There were men perched on the walls. They held bows and wore helmets. My heart beat faster—they looked like the men who'd taken Merlin from me.

I got close and saw that the wall was set with an enormous iron gate.

Another door, I thought unhappily. *I don't suppose if I scratch they'll let me in.* My eye caught a soldier looking down at me from the top of the wall and I froze. Would he yell the alarm, or shoot me dead on the spot?

The soldier raised his hands high, took a deep breath, and yawned.

"They're only guarding against men," I assured myself. "Not dogs."

I nosed the iron gate, looking for a way to slip inside. The bars crossed each other in a hash and were too tight for a dog my size.

But magic had opened a door for me at Merlin's house. Maybe it would here too.

Fire! Ice blast! Explosions of shock! I thought with intensity.

Nothing happened.

Magic door-opening spell!

My Asteria hung from my neck, glowing too faintly to notice. And the gate still stood, casting crossed shadows on the grass inside the castle yard, where Merlin's scent trail lay.

Stupid door.

* * *

Sounds perked my ears. I'd been sitting sadly at the gate for some time, but I spun to attention.

Barking. Playful yaps. Rustling of leaves.

Branches burst open at the tree-lined edge of the forest behind me, spilling forth a pack of rowdy, rambunctious dogs.

"Dogs!" I said, leaping forward, racing toward the action.

"Yap! Yap! Woof! Grrrr!" Their noises made my ears happy. Their smells were like treats. I hadn't been near dogs since I was little and under the deck with my brothers and sisters.

It was an enormous pack, easily twenty of them. They ran and tumbled and played with each other.

"Hello!" I cried to them. "Hello!"

They stopped playing. Ears lifted and snouts turned. They spotted me. "WOOF! WOOF! WOOF!"

They barked, friendly and curious. These weren't shy, scared dogs. But they were also typical, in that they couldn't talk. I'd gotten too used to having my Asteria.

"Woof! Woof!" I barked back in a friendly tone. I pressed my ears to my head and lowered my neck to show respect. My tail wagged low and slow.

I still spoke dog very well.

The pack rushed around me in a flurry. Tails wagged and

74

snouts jockeyed for the honor of sniffing my rear end and underbelly.

After the dogs approved me, I turned my nose on them. There's a lot you can learn from a dog's backside. Besides their unique scent, you can tell how well they're eating, their age, and if they're healthy. But even with all that, not even the most loving human will ever sniff a dog's butt. They don't know what they're missing

I could tell that these dogs were healthy, young, and exercised.

"Are you a wild pack?" I asked a tall Irish hound who was nosing around my neck. "You finding good food in the forest?"

He cocked his head. *Right, no human speech.*

His chest was jingling, and I noticed a small tin tag hanging from a leather collar. I looked around and noticed that the dogs all had collars. I relied so much on my nose and ears, I sometimes forgot to look.

These were owned dogs, every one of them. There were beagles, shepherds, and terriers. On their coats I smelled hare and deer blood.

"All right, boys and girls, no more dawdling!" cried a voice. Tree branches snapped and twigs crackled under the weight of a trio of horses and riders that strode out of the forest. Three tall men in hats sat on heavy stallions.

One man put his fingers in his mouth and blew a high

whistle. The entire pack whipped to attention, filing into line behind the riders. They left me exposed and alone on the grass. The men riding the horses wore the same clothing as those who had attacked our house. One shot me an angry look.

"In line!" he shouted.

Instinctively, I bolted into the group of dogs following the horses.

He thinks I'm one of the pack, I realized. My Asteria glowed so dimly, it looked like a tag on a collar.

"Hunt's coming back!" a soldier shouted from the wall. He turned toward the castle and raised both hands above his head.

The iron gate groaned. It slowly fell toward us, two thick cables easing its way down.

They were opening the front door! I kept close behind the horses, amazed at my good luck. The scent of blood made me look up, and I noticed the body of a deer laid over a horse's back. Another rider had a dozen dead rabbits tied to his saddle. This group had been hunting, and now the guards were welcoming them home.

We tromped over the iron gate, and the horses' metal shoes clattered against the bars. The dogs in the pack were panting tiredly, but I sensed a stir of excitement, as if something wonderful were about to happen.

Deep in the scrum of dogs, I lowered my snout to the grass and sorted through the hundreds of scents. Dogs, horses, men, leather, flour, chickens, sheep, cow's milk, wood, and iron. It was a labyrinth of smells. My mind raced between them, separating the individual aromas from the hundreds.

A wooden door creaked open to my left and distracted me.

"Breakfast is on, my wild ones!" a burly voice shouted. My ears twitched at the word:

Breakfast.

I turned and saw dogs stream through the doorway of a large wooden structure about twice the size of Merlin's house. Delicious smells wafted out: bran bread, chicken, and bone marrow.

I caught up with the tail end of the pack and pushed my way inside. The sun in the castle yard had been hot, but this wooden house was dark and cool, with just slivers of light leaking in between the roof boards.

Dogs leapt at a big, bearded man. He pushed them down affectionately. "All right! All right!" he said, knocking the top off a great barrel and hefting it in the air. "Here you go!"

Expertly, he dumped the contents of the barrel into a long trough that ran the length of the wooden house. Dogs scrambled across the straw-laden floor and dunked their heads into what was a river of chunky food.

I was one of them; my instinct to eat forced out every other thought. Food was in my mouth. Bone marrow enriched the grain meal, and its meaty taste filled my cheeks.

Food! Food! Food!

None of the dogs fought. We each had more than enough. When it was finally gone, each overstuffed one of us licked the juice from the wooden trough until all we could taste was the oak. I joined a group at one of the many tin bowls of fresh water and lapped it up until my gut stretched uncomfortably.

Satisfied, I wagged my tail at the pack and turned to the door of the house.

It was closed.

The bearded man was nowhere in sight. Faint light trickled into the doghouse. I hadn't noticed the big man leave.

I scratched at the door and barked.

Fire! Ice blast! Shock! I thought.

Magical door-opening spell!

I was trapped, with Merlin's scent trail right outside. My hunger had led me astray.

I turned and saw that the other dogs were all as overstuffed as I was, but they were content, settling down into piles of soft hay and dozing.

Seeing them made me realize how exhausted I was myself. I hadn't slept in a day and a night. So I dropped into a bed of straw and found myself drifting away.

For as much as I'd eaten, I felt empty inside.

12

The Poop Boy

I WOKE UP MUCH LATER. NO MORE SUN STREAMED THROUGH THE roof. Moonlight seeped in, casting a silvery haze over all the dogs.

I got up and stretched my legs. My body ached all over. A full day and night of travel really hurt.

A floppy-eared shepherd walked over and sniffed my neck. I lowered my ears and wagged my tail at him. Then some of the other dogs who were awake came over and surrounded me. A young terrier nosed me under the chin. They were letting me into the pack.

These dogs were living a good life. But I knew my home was elsewhere.

There was a noise outside the kennel. The dogs turned and wagged their tails. Others woke up and perked their ears. A dozen furry heads were rising from the straw.

The wooden door clicked, and the whole pack rushed it, making a terrific scrum around the entrance. The door pushed open into the crowd of dogs, and a small boy slipped his head through.

"Hello! Hello!" he called out in a friendly whisper. "Would you make some room?" He shooed back a tall wolf-hound and gently moved a beagle aside with his foot. The boy pushed his way inside, trailing a small shovel and a wooden bucket in his back hand. I charged into the pack, going for the open door, but got jammed between a pair of furry butts. The boy shut the door with his foot.

"Now, you can't bark," the boy said, putting his finger to his lips. "Sit, all of you. Sit! Sit!"

Amazingly, every dog did as they were told. The boy set aside the shovel and bucket and pulled a small leather pouch from his vest. "Nighttime treats!" he said with a grin. The dogs wiggled impatiently.

"Sturdy, Whitefoot, Hardy, Bo, Jakke, Tarri," he said, dropping a morsel of chicken into each dog's mouth. "Hemmerli, Aura, Troy, Amiable, Clenche," he continued through the pack. He fed every dog and called them by name.

After they got their treat, each dog walked back to their sleeping place. The boy patted them as they went, and most turned to lick his hand.

He fed the last of the dogs: "Bragge, Ringwood, Hold-fast. Good dogs!"

The boy stopped short when he came to me. He shook

out his pouch, but it was empty. "Sorry, boy," he said. "You must be new. I only bring just enough."

He knelt down and gave me a good looking-at. I sniffed him.

He was young, maybe Morgana's age, and not in the best health. I could tell he was underfed and had just gotten over being sick. The smell of human waste was on his clothes, a great variety of it. His hair was light, even in the dark kennel, and his eyes were kind.

"You're a funny-looking one. . . ." The boy reached out and rubbed his hand across my neck. "I like your mane, so fluffy." My Asteria chain was hidden within my fur, but I was afraid he'd feel it, so I tensed. Then something familiar caught my nose.

"You're tickling me!" the boy laughed as I sniffed around his elbows and hands. Deep in the folds of his palms, I found the scent I was looking for.

"You've been with Merlin!" I said, jumping on his chest and pressing my snout to his face. The boy's eyes widened, and his smile twisted into a grimace. "I can smell him on you! Tell me where they have him! I've been looking all day and night!"

The boy flailed his arms and knocked me back, nearly falling over himself. "Please don't! Please don't!" he cried. "Help me! Help!"

The pack went to high alert. They barked and woofed

madly. None of them knew what was wrong, but their boy was alarmed, so they were too.

"Don't be afraid!" I said as I tried to get near him, but howling dogs blocked my path.

"Help!" the boy screamed. "Help me, please!"

He wouldn't listen to me. Humans were afraid of a dog that spoke. I had to remember that.

There was another noise at the door. It swung wide open, and the burly, bearded man charged in with a crazed expression.

"There a wolf in here?" he shouted, brandishing a wooden club and scanning the pack. He looked at the terrified boy. "Where's the wolf?"

"No!" the boy screamed. "It's a dog! It's one of the dogs." He pointed his shaking finger in my direction, and the bearded man spotted me.

"Quiet!" he commanded, snapping his fingers. Instantly, every dog went silent and sat down.

"He got the madness? He's not foaming," the bearded man said, pointing the club at me.

"No," the boy answered. "He . . . he talked."

The big man's head jerked a little. He wheeled around and faced the boy. "He *what?*"

"He talked, Kennel Master," the boy said. "He's a demon or a spirit." The boy's eyes shot wildly between me and the big man.

The kennel master screwed up his face into a scowl. "Arthur, what on earth are you talking about?"

"He sp-spoke, Kennel Master. I s-swear it," said the boy, whose name I'd just learned was Arthur. "S-see for yourself."

The kennel master grumbled and turned to me. He crouched down and leaned low, right in my face. "You a demon, dog? Hmm? Got anything to *say* for yourself?"

Humans were scared of a talking dog, and this one had a club. So I decided that I didn't.

"Looks like he's not talking!" the kennel master yelled at Arthur. "Fill that bucket, poop boy. I'm going back to bed."

He turned and the dogs cleared a path for him.

"But, Kennel Master—" Arthur started.

"Not another peep."

The big man slammed the door.

The pack dogs were still on alert. Arthur stood in the corner, panting heavily, leaning against the wall. I stayed on the floor, giving him my most innocent puppy eyes. I didn't want him to scream again.

After a while the other dogs relaxed and started settling in the hay. Arthur looked at me warily.

"You did speak, didn't you?" he said in a small voice. I wagged my tail to show him I meant no harm. "Are you a demon?" he asked. I stopped wagging and whined through my nose. "Are you a spirit?" he asked, and I made a crying sound. The boy stopped leaning against the wall and took a step toward me. "What are you, then?"

"I'm a dog," I said, lifting my ears. The boy spasmed backward. "Please, please don't shout," I said, standing. "I'm Merlin's dog. He was stolen and brought to this castle, and I smell him on you. Do you know where he is?"

"You're . . . Merlin's dog? The old man they've got?"

"Yes, my name is Nosewise."

He nodded slowly, looking vaguely horrified. "How is it *you talk?*"

"This magic stone around my neck. It's called an Asteria," I answered, lifting my chin so he could see.

Arthur's mouth was dry and his lips made smacking noises. "Merlin didn't mention a talking dog was looking for him," he said.

"The talking is new, and Merlin doesn't know I'm here."

"So he really is a *wizard*," the boy said, almost to himself.

"Yes! He's very good."

"I thought he was a crazy old man,"

"So you spoke to him?" I asked, a little too excitedly. "Where is he?"

"Quiet down, or you'll bring back the kennel master," Arthur said. I flattened my ears and tried to calm myself. "He's in the tower."

"Are you one of the soldiers?" I asked, growing suspicious.

"No, I'm the waste handler. Or the poop boy, as you can

see they call me. I clean the chamber pots and the dogs' kennels, too."

"Ahh," I said more quietly. "So *that's* why you smell like that."

"Thanks for noticing," Arthur said in an irritated tone. I got the feeling that I'd offended him, so I decided to pay him a compliment.

"They must respect you a lot," I said. "To let you handle all the poop."

Arthur smirked grimly. "As surprising as it might be for a dog, it's not a good title. It's the worst job there is. But I have access to most of the rooms, and that's how I met Merlin." His eyebrows twitched as though remembering something unpleasant. "His chamber pot was, uh, *characteristic* of a man his age."

"So he's still here?"

"Last I checked this morning."

"And what about Morgana? A girl about as old as you."

"Someone said Lord Destrian had a girl with him. But I'm not allowed in his rooms."

"Can you take me to Merlin, Arthur? Please!" I begged him. "Lord Destrian took away his Asteria. He's powerless without magic. But if I bring him this"—I stretched up my chin to reveal the stone—"he can be a wizard again. I don't know how to use it, but Merlin's a master. Once his magic's back, he can get us out of here!"

That piqued Arthur's interest. "You sure?"

"Positive!" I answered. "Why else would they take his Asteria away? They know they can't keep him if he has it!"

"Really," Arthur said. "And could he get me out as well?"

"You want to leave? Isn't your family here?"

"No," Arthur said, flinching. "I'm a ward of Lord Destrian."

"A ward? That's like a pet. No, not a pet! You're an apprentice! Lord Destrian is your master?"

"I'm not an apprentice. Cleaning up night soil isn't a trade that you have to learn. I'm more of a slave, if you ask me. When you don't have family in these parts, you become a ward and the lord does what he wants with you."

"Lord Destrian is *a bad master?*"

"Yes, very bad," Arthur said. "I've been trying to find a way out for ages."

"I had a bad master too!"

"Did you? Stars . . . I'm talking to a dog." Arthur slapped his palm against his forehead. "This is insane."

"Merlin could help you. He took me away from my bad master."

"Right, I'm sure you and I have a lot in common."

"It's true. Merlin's a good man and a good master. If you help me bring this stone to him—he'll get us *all* out of here."

Arthur peered down at me warily. "I just have to take you to him?"

"I give him the stone and he magics us away!"

"Well, you know, poop boy does come with some powers," Arthur said, pulling a ring of jangling keys from his belt. "Most of the castle's asleep. If we head there now, maybe no one will catch us."

"Yes!" I said, hopping for joy and giving Arthur a lick. Despite what he said, I thought he smelled *wonderful*.

Arthur pushed me away from him. "Calm, boy. They don't lock you in a tower when they want it to be *easy* to break you out."

13

The Giant Knight

"THIS IS THE SERVANTS' ENTRANCE," ARTHUR SAID, FLICKING through a set of keys at the far side of the yard. "It should be the safest way."

We entered a dark hallway, but I could follow the scent of human footsteps. Men and women of all ages had walked here, and each sniff told me something. One woman was pregnant. An old man had a bad cut. A young girl ate way too much garlic.

"Nosewise, heel," Arthur said, grasping me in the dark. "You have to be very quiet."

I heard a creak, and a sliver of flickering light filled the hallway. Arthur had opened a door into a room full of sleeping people. There were a dozen beds with men and women wrapped in dirty sheets.

I thought *Merlin's* snoring was bad.

"Oh, what's this?" A ruddy-faced woman was sitting up

in bed. "Arthur," she said, "what business do you have coming through here this late?"

"Sorry, Miss Flanagan," Arthur whispered, ushering me forward.

"You're lucky I can't sleep or you would've woken me up," the old woman said. "Hey! Everyone!" she shouted to the sleeping people around her. "Look at Arthur traipsing through in the middle of the night!"

Several unhappy faces woke up blinking.

"Don't shout!" Arthur whispered, putting his finger to his lips. "Nosewise, let's go!" He grabbed me and we bounded toward a door on the other side.

"Idiot boy!" she yelled, waking up the rest. "People are trying to sleep!"

We traveled more hallways, pantries, kitchens, and sleeping places. Each was dingy, dark, and damp. We trekked up a rickety set of wooden steps and Arthur placed a key into yet another door.

When he opened it, the world seemed to change. We entered a room larger than any I'd ever seen. The walls and floor sparkled. Crystals hung from the ceiling on steel chains; soft sofas and polished wood tables sat on thick carpets. Brightly burning torches were fixed to the walls every few steps.

In the middle of the room stood a large brass statue of a solder with a winged helmet. It looked like Lord Destrian.

"This is the castle proper, where our betters live," Arthur said.

"Your 'betters'?" I asked. "Better than you at what?"

"Better at being people, of course," Arthur said flatly. "You saw how they make us live. When I get out, maybe I can work on a farm or in a shop. Anything but cleaning up left-behinds."

"Maybe you can live with Merlin and me!"

"With a wizard? Talking dogs and magic rocks?" Arthur laughed.

"Fine," I answered, feeling offended. "It was just a thought."

My nails clicked on the tiles, and the torchlight reflected in the brass statue. Lord Destrian stood tall in his armor, and his face was just how I remembered it, thick-lipped with a strong brow. He didn't look much like Morgana. Nor the figure who had appeared in the leaves.

"Shaped by the finest metalsmiths in the realm," Arthur said. "Lord Destrian glorifies himself at great expense."

"Metalsmiths?" I asked. Something wasn't right. The statue looked bronze, but there was no scent of metal. I smelled the armored foot. "This is made of oak."

"No, it's brass," Arthur said, coming up beside me. He

flicked the calf of the statue with his fingernail, and it rang like metal.

"Lord Destrian knows magic too." I sniffed again, just to make certain. "It looks and sounds like metal, but he forgot to make it smell right. Morgana called that a *glamour*."

"Your stone's glowing," Arthur said nervously.

"Maybe it feels the magic," I said, looking down at it. "What do you know about Lord Destrian? Morgana says he's her father. She's one of Merlin's pets like me. No! She's an *apprentice*. And that's something different!"

"I only know what everyone knows," Arthur said, looking up at the statue. "His family ruled these lands for centuries, and from what I've heard, ruled them kindly. But after the king died, he changed. Destrian became cruel and claimed all the forests and rivers for a hundred miles."

"And he knows magic," I added. "When he attacked our house, he had these flying worms that ate Merlin's spells."

"Really?" Arthur said, turning white. "Let's hurry."

We crossed the great room and stopped at a set of iron doors. Arthur paused to pick his way through the ring of keys.

Arthur was frightened of magic, but he had power too. I wished I had keys and hands for using them.

"Destrian keeps honored guests in the highest room of the tower," Arthur said, putting the proper key into the lock. "Also *prisoners* he wishes to treat as guests."

The lock clicked, and the door swung open into a bright room lit with torches. Woven tapestries hung from the walls, and a great stone staircase spiraled up at the opposite end. I caught a scent on the floor. Merlin passed through here, and Morgana, too.

"Eh! You there! What you doing?" said a voice, startling us.

A leather-armored man stood against the wall. He wore a sword on his hip and grabbed an oak club off a table.

"Oh, g-guardsman . . ."

"Yeah, good evening to you," said the man in a nasty voice. "Answer my question."

Arthur looked panicked. "H-here to clean the pots. For the man at the—the top floor."

"Oh right, the poop boy," the guard said, smiling. His scent was familiar to me. "And why the dog?" the guardsman asked, pointing the cudgel. "You gonna feed it to him?"

"N-no, he's a—a tracking dog. Trained to sniff for contraband." Arthur was good at telling lies. "It's something new the kennel master's trying. He wants him to search the wizard's room."

"Without an escort?" the guard asked.

Arthur glanced down at me, at a loss for what to say. I lowered my neck and flared my nostrils. Arthur nodded.

"Just a quick sniff," he said, taking my hint. "It will only be a few minutes. Come on, boy."

"Not a good time," the guardsman said, stepping in front of Arthur.

"This is what the k-kennel master told me to do. His orders came from Lord Destrian himself!" My ears perked at that. I didn't know Arthur had such guts.

"Is that right?" the guardsman replied. "Well, let's ask him about it when he comes back down."

"When he comes back down?"

"Yeah. Lord Destrian is up with the wizard now." The guard's eyes narrowed. "Probably working him over. Been there hours. Not sure why he brought the girl."

I recognized this man's scent. He was one of the soldiers who had attacked our house. I noticed him leaning on his right leg. He was one of the three Merlin had frozen to the ground.

"Now get out of here, you turnip!" The guard spat and raised his cudgel. "I'm tired of you!"

"All right!" Arthur stepped back. "Come on, Nosewise."

I stood firm before the soldier. I knew exactly who he was.

"Don't talk that way to my friend," I said through gritted, growling teeth.

The guardsman's eyes went wide. "Wha—what?"

"I said, don't talk to him—and get out of our way!" I barked at the man. "Woof! Woof! I'm a demon!" I shouted. "A scary dog demon and I'm going to bite you!"

"Ahhh!" The guardsman screamed, dropped his cudgel to the floor, and rushed for the opposite wall of the room. He grabbed a cord that hung from hooks and snaked its way into the stones. He pulled it hard, and bells rang throughout the castle. "Intruders in the tower!" he shouted.

Clanging bells reverberated down the halls. I turned to Arthur and shouted, "Come on!"

The boy looked terrified. "Come now!" I said. "Merlin can save us!"

Arthur ran to me, shaking head to toe.

"Don't go near that demon!" the guardsman shouted, and grabbed one of the fiery torches off the wall. He hurled it at me, and the burning bulb crashed into my snout, knocking me down to the stones.

In my daze I saw that the fiery tip was resting on my chest, sprouting flames. Arthur ran and kicked the torch off me. He picked me up and charged up the stairs of the tower. The world bounced and spun around me.

Partway up the twisting stone staircase, I felt my eyes snap back into focus. Arthur was struggling with my weight; I'm sure I was half as heavy as him. The torch-lit walls slowly revolved as Arthur trudged up the spiral staircase.

"Put me down," I said, kicking. His fingers loosened, and I dropped to the blocky stairs.

"Are you all right?"

"Yeah," I said. The impact of the thrown torch had been enough to cross my eyes but the flames hadn't hurt. I glanced down at my chest; my mane was unburned, not even a singe.

"I can make it on my own," I said, and leapt up the stairs. Arthur gasped and charged behind.

Up and up we went, an endless spiral of stones sliding down around us. Alarm bells sounded below. Faintly, I heard men's panicked voices.

"There's the door," Arthur whispered. He came up behind me and put his hand on my back so I would let him go ahead. The stairway had grown narrow, and now it was barely wide enough for two men to walk shoulder to shoulder. The stairs steepened and led up into what looked like the ceiling.

No, not the ceiling. The light was dim and made it hard to see. There was a trapdoor above us, blocking off the top of the stairs. Arthur crept up the last few steps below it. From his belt he took the ring of keys, holding them together in one hand so they wouldn't jingle.

"Is this the door to the—"

Arthur held his finger to his lips. "The only room in the tower," he whispered, pointing above.

Merlin was up there, along with Lord Destrian and Morgana. Had they heard the bells? Were they expecting an attack?

If they were, they were thinking about knights and soldiers, not a dog with a magic stone. I could surprise them, run to Merlin, and give him the Asteria. All I had to do was put it in his hands.

While Arthur sorted through the keys, I turned my ears to the room above. I didn't hear anything.

"Just get me in," I whispered. "I'll do the rest."

Arthur nodded. He slipped the key into the door above his head. The lock clicked. Arthur heaved, throwing open the heavy wooden door. I charged up the last few steps, my Asteria bouncing against my chest.

"Merlin!" I shouted, launching myself into the room. "Take the Asteria!"

My words bounced back to me from the gray stone walls. I was standing in the room alone.

14

The Mysterious Tower

ARTHUR PEEKED HIS HEAD THROUGH THE TRAPDOOR. HIS EYES were wide and his breath was short. "Where . . . ?"

"They're not here."

"What happened?" Arthur grabbed the floor and pulled himself up. "The guard said they were—"

"Yes, they were here. I can smell them. Merlin, Morgana, and Destrian. The scent's a few hours old."

"So they left?" Arthur asked. "Without the soldier downstairs knowing?"

I dipped my head through the trapdoor and sniffed the stairs. The scents were there, too, but faded. If they'd gone back down, the smell would be stronger.

"They escaped some other way."

I glanced around the room. It was wide and circular. At one end there was a bed with rumpled sheets and a wooden desk heavy with scrolls. Two long chains were attached to the wall.

"That's where they had Merlin locked up," Arthur said.

He peeked over the rim of a black pot that sat beside the bed and winced. "Needs to be changed."

The walls of the room were bare apart from a large fireplace heaped with burning wood. The flames licked up high and hot, sometimes spilling smoke into the little chamber. Smoky wisps pooled on the ceiling, maybe twenty feet above our heads. They streamed out a small, moonlight-filled window.

"Could they have gone up there?"

"Through the window?" Arthur asked, incredulous. It was small and nearly as high as the ceiling. "Climbing what? A rope? Why wouldn't they use the front gate?"

"I don't know. But they didn't go downstairs."

Men's voices echoed up from below. Even Arthur could hear them. He flipped the heavy trapdoor closed. "It doesn't lock from this side. Nosewise, we're trapped in here!"

I scurried across the room, sniffing all I could. The well-stuffed bed was made of straw. Merlin had slept there through a fitful night. I put my forepaws on the desk and checked its surface. He'd sat there for a while but hadn't touched the scrolls. One was unrolled slightly, and though I couldn't read the words, I saw a picture painted at the top of the parchment. It was a sword drawn in shiny gold paint.

I smelled the chains that sprouted from the walls and noticed that they ended in iron cuffs. On the inside, I sensed flakes of skin that had rubbed off Merlin's wrists.

"Was he chained here when you saw him this morning?"

Arthur was shaking on top of the trapdoor. He looked up at me like he'd forgotten who I was.

"Arthur, tell me!"

"Yes, they had him chained," he answered.

Why chain a man to the wall if he's in a locked room? I thought. *Merlin is old; he can't fight back.*

Half a dozen footfalls echoed up the staircase. Arthur heard them too, and looked at me.

"Heave!" The trapdoor beneath Arthur's feet jumped, knocking the boy off balance. He dropped down hard on his knees, catching a few thick fingers that had shot up between the door and the floor. A grown man screamed, and the fingers withdrew.

"Nosewise!" Arthur called.

Why chain a man in a locked room? I thought again. There was no place to escape. Only a high window and a red-hot fireplace. Had they gone up the chimney in a puff of smoke?

I remembered the torch the guard had thrown at me. The flames had been bright—but they hadn't burned me.

"It's an illusion!" I shouted to Arthur. "More illusion magic!"

I raced across the tiny chamber, toward the burning fireplace. The heat flared against my face, but I ignored it.

"What are you doing?" Arthur shouted.

"Heave!" cried the voice from below. The trapdoor exploded up and the boy tumbled onto his side. His eyes were wide with terror when he saw me—standing smack in the center of the furnace.

"The fire's an illusion," I said, warm flames licking up the sides of my face. "Come on!"

Snarling soldiers with swords and iron hats poured up the staircase. They, too, saw me engulfed in the blaze. And they froze.

"Arthur!" I shouted again. The boy glanced at the men with their blades and charged into the fireplace with me, covering his face and disappearing behind.

"He is a demon!" one soldier said. "He stands in flame."

"That's right!" I answered, withdrawing into the fire, growling low and spookily. "I'll drag you in too!"

Behind the fire was a tiny room. Arthur was huddled in the corner, patting himself down, checking for burns. He had none. The fire was a trick, just like Destrian's statue had been. This castle was made of magical secrets.

Arthur couldn't catch his breath, but he pointed behind. "L-look!" he whispered as loud as he dared. There was another staircase—this one leading down.

15

Two for the Road

AT THE BOTTOM OF THE STAIRS IT WAS VERY DARK—NO LIGHT but the faint glow of my Asteria.

"Why a secret passage?" I asked, dipping my nose to the stony floor. Merlin, Lord Destrian, and Morgana had all come this way, but without any guards.

"I don't know," Arthur said. "The stones are cold, even colder than the cellar gets. So we're underground."

Then he stopped walking.

"You know, you really did look like a demon," he said. "Going into the fire like that."

"I'm a dog, Arthur," I said, lifting my tail and exposing my backside. "Give me a whiff if you don't believe me!"

Arthur held up his hand. "I take you at your word."

The tunnel was damp and sloped downward. Along the way, I explained the types of magic I knew about: elemental, illusion, and alchemy. Arthur was baffled by it all, and I couldn't really explain it. The only magic I'd done was accidentally blowing up a door. The memory made my tail wag. *Stupid door.*

Something sounded above my head. "What was that?"

Arthur whipped around. "Is someone here?" he shouted.

"I hear running water," I said, looking at the ceiling. Arthur gripped his chest and glowered at me.

After we'd walked a long while down the dark passageway, silvery light seeped into the tunnel. I lifted my nose and caught a whiff of trees and woods. The tunnel sloped upward. The light grew stronger; it was moonlight. Shadows stretched before us. The tunnel was opening into a forest of midnight trees.

"It's leading us out of the castle," Arthur said, amazed.

"If Lord Destrian wanted to take Merlin and Morgana somewhere, why not go out the front gate?"

"It's leading us *out* of the *castle*!" Arthur repeated, picking up his pace. We exited beneath a giant boulder that jutted into a thick grouping of trees, rocks, and grass.

Arthur hopped from foot to foot. "We're out! We're free!" I wagged my tail at his happy dance. It was good to be outside, but my goal was my family. I put my nose to the soil and picked out their scents.

"It seems they had three horses here. They mounted them and went . . . this way!"

"All right, so we won't go that way, then," Arthur said, peering at the trees.

I turned around with perked ears. "But that's where Merlin and Morgana went."

"And Destrian," Arthur said. "I can't go that way. He'll recapture me."

My ears pressed to my head. Arthur only wanted to escape the castle. I remembered that now.

"Well," I sighed, "thank you for your help." It had been nice having a pack mate again.

"Now, wait!" Arthur called out behind me. "You don't even know where you are!"

"On the way to my family."

"But this isn't a safe place to be. If you were right, and you heard water above us in the tunnel, then I think we passed under the river, and this is the Haunted Forest."

"The *Haunted* Forest?"

"That's not its real name," Arthur said. "It's called Grimmshode. But people *avoid* this side of the river." He stopped and looked down at the ground. "No towns nearby, really. Nowhere to go. Unless I cross south. But the soldiers patrol down there; they might catch me."

Arthur pressed his palms to his eyes.

I felt my tail wagging and had to force it still. "You know," I said, trying not to sound too pushy about it, "you *could* come with me and find Merlin. I'm sure he'd reward you."

Arthur looked at me from behind his hands. "Reward?"

"Yes," I said. "Bones! Back scratches! Tummy rubs!" Arthur crinkled his brow. "Or the kinds of things you like!"

"But they've gone into Grimmshode. *Spirits* live here. And the Fae don't like intruders."

"The Fae?"

"Otherworlders . . . monsters that walk the woods."

"Why would Lord Destrian bring Merlin and Morgana there?" I asked. "And alone—without soldiers?"

"I should know the mind of a madman?"

The whole thing made my tail twitch. But it didn't matter where they'd gone. I would follow them anywhere.

"Can that charm of yours protect you?" Arthur asked. He looked frightened but hopeful.

"I don't think so," I said, shaking the Asteria on the chain. "The only time it ever worked was an accident."

Arthur grimaced. "Then I suppose we must pray for lucky accidents."

"We?" I asked, my ears perking.

Arthur sighed. "For a little while. First safe town I find, I'm staying."

My tail wagged wildly, though I tried to keep it still. Arthur and I made our way into the wood. I had a pack mate again.

PART III

16

The Otherworld

WE WALKED THE WOODS STRAIGHT INTO MORNING. I KEPT MY nose to the ground, following all three scents and making sure they didn't separate.

"Are you sure we're still on the right path?" Arthur asked, bleary-eyed. The sun was rising through the trees and casting hazy rays.

"Positive," I answered, licking my nose. "Tracking's tougher at night, but now the ground is warming and the smells are buzzy and sharp. All you have to do is sniff!"

"Maybe that's all *you* have to do," Arthur said.

"I wish you could smell them too," I said, wagging my tail. "Wouldn't that be nice?"

Arthur laughed woozily. "No. At the castle, I spent all day cleaning chamber pots—I'd be happy never to smell again!"

I stopped in my tracks. *How could he say such a thing?*

"You could have learned *so much* from that poop," I said. Arthur looked surprised by my tone, but this was something

I took seriously. "Merlin was just like you—when I brought deer cakes in the house, he got really upset. And he missed out on a whole lot of—"

"Nosewise, it was a bad job. You have to believe me."

"But that's because you spent all your time *worrying*. If you would just give it a *taste* you'd find—"

"Nosewise, I'm going to be sick!" Arthur shouted, stomping away from me.

I watched him crunch through the leaves and grab hold of a tree. He bent over and breathed hard while clutching his tummy.

I'll never understand humans.

Some hours later I felt a tugging at my neck.

"Nosewise, the stone," Arthur said, pointing.

I looked down and saw that my Asteria was acting strangely.

"What's happening?"

The Asteria was lifted and straining ahead. "It's pointing down the scent trail."

"Is it Merlin pulling it?" Arthur asked.

"I don't know! Maybe!"

My tail wagged at the thought, and I picked up my pace.

We'd been traveling a long time, but the Asteria gave us new energy. Trees and boulders went by us in a blur. As we went farther down the trail, the stone pulled harder. We were getting close to something!

Up ahead, the forest was thinning. Then it opened up into a clearing.

Arthur and I stopped running. We stood inside a perfect circle of treelessness. Almost like inside the Wall of Trees back home, it was devoid of everything but dirt and dead leaves.

"Oh no," Arthur said.

"Why don't trees grow here?"

"Nothing grows here," Arthur answered. He took a backward step.

"What is it?"

"A place we need to leave," Arthur said, gesturing for me to come away.

"But Merlin came through here."

"That's unfortunate for him," Arthur answered. "Because I don't think he made it back out."

He pointed to the ground, and I saw something growing there: a circle of mushrooms standing in the dirt. Their caps were all sizes, shapes, and colors. None that I recognized.

"Don't go near that!" Arthur shouted.

Before I had a chance to heed his warning, the force that had been tugging my Asteria increased. The chain slipped over my head, and the stone soared into the center of the mushroom circle. I barked, wordless, and leapt after it. Arthur caught my hind leg, and I watched the stone blink into nothingness in midair.

"It's a faerie ring!" Arthur shouted, wrapping his arms across my belly and dragging me to the ground. "It's a portal! A door to the Otherworld!"

I barked at him in protest.

"Your voice?" he said.

I turned back to the faerie ring and yipped.

"You can't go in there for it. You'll be trapped in the Otherworld. It's where wood spirits come from—the monsters that walk the forest."

I blinked at Arthur. He looked terrified.

"Something evil lives in there."

The air at the center of the mushroom circle seemed to swirl and bend.

"Destrian has some mad plan for Merlin," Arthur said, throwing up his arms. "He's thrown him into the Otherworld or—like a fool—gone himself! There's no saving him now. We have to—"

I thrashed in Arthur's arms and broke free. "Nosewise, no!" Arthur shouted as I ran toward the portal. The scents tracked right to the edge.

"Don't go in there! Come with me instead!" Arthur shouted. "We'll find a safe place together. You'll be my dog, and I'll take care of you."

I turned and looked at Arthur. He didn't understand. I wasn't chasing Merlin and Morgana to have someone look after me.

Arthur's hands were outstretched and shaking. I barked and wagged my tail at him. Then I jumped into the center of the circle.

I was looking after *them*.

17

Do All Tree Men Talk Funny?

IT FELT AS IF THERE WAS A THICK SPIDERWEB STRETCHING ACROSS my face. My whiskers folded back and my ears flattened.

Pop!

My eyes opened, and I was in a moonlit forest.

It had *just* been daylight. But hazy stars peeked between the treetops. Every rock and blade of grass glowed with an inner light, making everything visible but strange.

I saw the faerie ring beside me. Its mushrooms were shimmering now. Arthur was nowhere to be seen.

Did I cross into another world?

I put my nose to the ground and sniffed for Merlin's scent. Nothing smelled quite the same. I circled the faerie ring twice and thought I found a hint of him, but the scent was unfamiliar in my nose.

Something chimed to my right. I turned and saw the silver chain resting in the grass. The Asteria glowed like a little moon, and I nosed it, trying to get the chain around my neck.

Sharp pain pierced my snout and I jumped. There was some needle in my nose! I shook my head and sneezed.

Two bright specks of dust shot out. They looked like little fireflies.

I blinked at them. They twinkled and floated down to my Asteria. I barked to warn them off, but they grabbed the chain somehow and raised it in the air. With each holding a link and the Asteria hanging below, there was a natural hole for my head.

I slid my neck through and instantly felt the change.

"Thank you," I said to the little lights. I couldn't tell if they were smart enough to understand. "What are you?"

They shivered and soared away from me, flying into the woods. Then they stopped, as if asking me to follow them.

Soon I was running through twinkling grass and between tree trunks that hummed with music. I caught glimpses of animals I'd never seen. Some had too many eyes, others were shaped impossibly, and all disappeared as soon as I spotted them.

Finally something delectable filled my nostrils. A fatty stew was cooking. I couldn't pick out any of the ingredients, but it made my mouth water.

The little flying lights guided me around an enormous boulder, and I stopped short.

Under a tree, a man was sitting, his legs crossed, next to a dying fire. A cook pot sat in the coals.

His hair was long and thick, rising off his forehead and covering broad shoulders. His eyebrows were sharp and long; black pupils filled his entire eyes. Blue light seemed to shimmer within the skin of his face and made him glow.

The dancing motes of dust flew to him and circled his ears. He turned to me and smiled with sharp teeth.

"Don't be scared of these little sprites. They mostly play and no one bites!" the man said, and I froze. It seemed like he had been expecting me.

"They keep an eye out for me when I'm in the wood: what comes, what goes, what's bad, what's good," he said in a friendly voice. "Any strange happenings that walk about, my little sprites will find them out!" The man looked young and strong, and even though he was hunched over the pot, I could see that he was very tall. "And you are strange, without a doubt!"

I panted nervously. Arthur had said spirits haunted the woods. "You talk funny," I said, shivering.

"I do? I do!" The man slapped his knee and laughed so hard it made me jump. "But so do you!" He pointed a long-nailed finger in my direction. "So sit with me and share my stew!"

His voice was kind, but there were strange growths on his forehead. They looked something like long antlers but were made of knotty wood.

He smiled wide and held his hand out, palm down. I stretched my neck so I could take a sniff. My nose brushed against his knuckle, and he giggled.

He smelled strange. The scents in this place still had me turned around. I didn't like not trusting my nose.

"Did I pass the test?" he asked. He held out a wooden bowl full of soup. "I've had my fill; you eat the rest."

"Thank you, sir," I said, and took a lap of the stew.

As I ate, he placed his palm gently on my neck and stroked me. I bristled at first, but his hand was firm. "That was good," I said when I finished the bowl. "Haven't eaten since yesterday."

"A dog that gives thanks," the big man said, and laughed. "You must be some noble's pet, and could teach *me* some manners yet."

"That's not me," I said.

"Well then, you are a farmer's dog." He looked at me, squinting. "And reject the crudeness of the hog."

"I don't live on a farm!"

"Then! Some *magician* you assist, or else how have you gotten *this?*" The man grabbed hold of my silver chain and slid his fingers to the stone.

I jumped away from him and barked. "Don't touch my Asteria. It's mine!"

"I guessed right!" he said, and smiled. "I won't take your stone. But why'd your master leave his dog alone?"

I felt my heart beat fast, and I was panting. "You're a stranger; I shouldn't talk to you. I don't even know where I am."

"Does magic scare you? Because *you* stepped through my magic door. *You* walked into my circle and found a place *you* weren't before. Where it's day in your realm, in mine it's night. If you go back through, it will be set right."

He sounded like he'd be sad to see me go.

"This is the realm of the Fae. These things are my sprites. Making offerings here is what I do this night. For I am a Fae of the wood, and I tend to my trees as a good Fae should."

"You're a tree man?" I asked.

He laughed. "A tree man? Yes."

"My name's Nosewise. I'm a dog."

He laughed again. "That was my guess."

"My master, Merlin, was kidnapped," I said, stepping close to him. "I followed his scent everywhere, through a castle and a forest. His trail led me to your magic door, but when I went through, I couldn't smell him anymore." Now *I* was speaking in rhyme—I shook it off. "Please tell me: have you seen him?"

The Tree Man was taken aback. He peered at me through slitted eyes and rubbed his chin with long-nailed fingers. "Merlin, you say. With a beard of gray? Tall knight and little girl leading the way?"

"That's them! Did you see which way they went?"

"Yes, I did see your party in my wood and rightly suspected it meant nothing good. The direction they went is my way too, so let me make a companion of you and guide you to your missing friend."

"Yes, let's go!" I barked, jumping on the Tree Man's knee. He smiled and roughly rubbed my ears.

"Just this way, around the bend."

"Magic comes from Summer," the Tree Man said as he walked me through the forest. "The Mothers turn the sun each day, and it in turn lights our way. They embolden the little nut in the earth to break the ground and show its worth, and grow into a towering tree. They beat the heart inside of me."

As we walked through the woods, the Tree Man gave me a lesson in magic.

"Are you familiar with the Mothers? Did your master give them heed?"

"Um, Merlin said that the Asteria brings what's inside of you out," I said. "He never talked about any . . . Mothers."

"Bah!" the Tree Man said, giving a dismissive wave. "No human respects the old ways anymore. Man wizards travel down the shore, giving magic shows for pennies and cheers. Real magic's been gone from *their* world for years."

"That's not true. Merlin's a great wizard."

"Respect for the old ways is key," the Tree Man said. "They are the source of all energy. It doesn't come from words or even your lovely stone. These tools only call to what's there; magic resides with *them* alone."

I trotted alongside him, struggling to keep pace with both the walk and the conversation.

"Well, can you show me? I've only done magic once before."

"Try something simple," the Tree Man said. He picked up a leaf from the ground. "Focus all of Nature's power and turn this leaf into a flower."

It was illusion magic he wanted. The same kind that was in Lord Destrian's castle.

"All right," I said. "I'll try."

My eyes closed and I held my breath. Then, in my Mind's Nose, I sensed what I wanted the leaf to become: one of the fragrant flowers Merlin grew in his garden.

I tried to focus, but my mind was filled with one awful thought: Merlin said magic wasn't for me. And I'd only ever cast a spell by accident.

I glanced shamefully at the Tree Man and sank to the forest floor.

He bent over and stroked my head. "You're more Talented than most men I see. Your problem is that you lack Certainty."

My ears perked at the word. "Certainty? Morgana wouldn't tell me what that was."

The Tree Man leaned back and smiled.

"A squirrel is Certain it's a squirrel. So it can climb a tree," he said. "A mirror is Certain it's a mirror. So it reflects an image of me. You are Certain you're a dog. So you can bark and run and bite. The moon is Certain it's the moon, and it lights our way at night.

"But Certainties are not forever. Everything will, one day, change. Some for worse and some for better. Some familiar, some strange." He held the leaf aloft in his fingers. "Someday this leaf will rot, turn to dirt, and be reborn as a flower. This is how each Mother expresses herself: by turning one thing into something else."

He set down the leaf on my forepaws. "We can mimic this process magically, if we do it with our Certainty. Now you must believe this leaf is a flower," the Tree Man said. "But it will help if you first think of something you are Certain of, like that the sun is hot or the sky is above."

"Something I'm Certain of?"

"Something that you *know* to be! And *that* will be your Certainty!"

I shook my head and thought of the thing I was most Certain of in the entire world:

Merlin is a good master.

In my Mind's Nose, I held the smell of his hair and his skin. I felt the soft touch of his hands on my ears and heard his happy laugh as I bounded out for our morning walk.

Merlin is a very good master.

"Now," the Tree Man said softly in my ear, "take that very Certain thought and let it roll over the spot in your mind that knows . . . this leaf is a beautiful rose."

I focused on my Certainty and felt calm for the first time in days. Then, just as Certain as I was that *Merlin is a very good master*, I was Certain the leaf was really a flower.

I opened my eyes. The leaf was still a leaf.

"Don't be disappointed," the Tree Man said. "Your attempt may be disjointed, but I've never seen an animal cast a spell. Now, perhaps that is very well the way things are meant to be. If I raised your hopes, please forgive me."

I smelled something unexpected and put my nose to the leaf. I took a whiff and my tail wagged.

"What is it?" the Tree Man said.

"The leaf!"

The Tree Man shot me a sideways glance and picked it up. He held it by the stem and spun it.

I pushed his hand with my snout. "Smell it!" I said. He gasped, knitting his brow beneath the oaky antlers.

"By the Mothers." He gave me a playful push. "It smells like one of your world's flowers! Fragrant as the height of May!"

I barked happily and jumped on his chest, licking his face.

"You have a Talent after all! There's much to learn! Let's swift, away!"

18

⌒⌒

The Fire Dancers

SOMEWHERE, DEEP IN THE WOODS, I HEARD CHIMING BELLS AND whistles.

"Ahh," sighed the Tree Man, "we've arrived."

I splayed my feet and lifted my ears. "Are we near Merlin?" I whispered.

The Tree Man nodded his head. "Your master we still pursue. But let me ask a favor of you." He gestured toward the music. "My people gather in these trees. Let's rest with them and take our ease."

"I don't know if I can stop. We don't want them to get away."

"You're the most intriguing creature that I've ever met, so much more than just a wizard's pet," the Tree Man said in a singing voice. "Come meet my people and share my fire too. And we will *help* you to do all that you aspire to."

My tail wagged at that. It would be good not to face Lord Destrian alone.

A steady drumbeat shook through the forest. The Tree Man walked with a skipping step. He dipped his graceful hands from side to side and cocked his head. He was doing a dance! I barked and ran in a circle. "I'm going to get you!" he cried playfully.

I waited for him to get near, then ran! He charged forward, leaping over logs and vines while I ducked under them. He was nearly as fast as me, but not quite. I spun around and he lunged at me; the two of us rolled in the dirt.

"We're here," he said.

I looked backward over the weeds and jumped to my feet.

All as far as my eyes could see, the forest was filled with dancing figures. Bonfires flamed ten feet high at the base of sparkling trees, and lithe men and women danced around them, touching hands.

"Your people?" I whispered.

Dozens of hammocks were strung between trees, and giggling children lounged in them together. A band of twelve men and women stood on a fallen log and played instruments loud and lively. One of them sang.

Summers wane and summers strain;
the summer's moving on

What dies the light and calms the sprite,
the summer's dead at dawn

Come ye! Come ye! And hear our woeful song!

Fight the fight and dance the night.
The summer's dead at dawn!

I followed the Tree Man out of the bramble and into the main throng of the party. A youngster whose face shone like the skin of an apple sat up and gasped. "King Oberon!" The Tree Man smiled and waved.

Others heard and turned their heads. A woman with leafy hair gave a smile full of sharp teeth. "King Oberon!" she called out. Dancers broke their lines and rushed to the Tree Man and me. They looked strange and frightening. "King Oberon!"

"King Oberon?" I said to the Tree Man, confused. He shrugged his shoulders and smiled.

There was a huge crowd around us. The trees above us in the grove seemed to wave their branches at him. The band sang. "Our king is home! Our king is home! And happy folks are we!"

"There's a lot of Fae here!" I said nervously. The Tree Man—Oberon—put his hand on my head without looking at me.

"My people! My people!" he cried. The chanting stopped and the musicians were still. The Fae had sharp cheekbones, dark eyes, and a strange glow to their skin. Some were tall and thin, some squat; others had growths on their eyebrows and arms like knotty wood.

"It pleases me greatly to return to my court. Oh, Fae of Summer, hear my report! We celebrate a future where we're free! Free from cold, and the Fae of old, and man's ceaseless villainy!"

> *The Great Mothers bless the Fae*
> *And curse the tribe of man*
> *They block their path and light our way*
> *To rule their oafish clan!*

The band sang, and the Fae grabbed each other's knotty hands and formed a dancing snake that slithered between bonfires.

I tried to work out what had been said, and what it meant.

"And who's this?" cried a throaty female voice behind me. "A traveler you picked up along the way?" A rough hand grabbed hold of my fur and made me jump.

I saw a light-haired Fae woman in a silk tunic lined with vines. Her features were sharp and frightening. Shadows seemed to crawl across her face. I blinked and realized that she was surrounded by three floating worms. One was wood-colored, the other black as night, and the third white like ash. They slithered about her head and neck without touching her, swimming through the air like water.

I yipped. They looked like the worms Lord Destrian had used to attack Merlin.

"Blodwen!" Oberon said, gripping her hand. "Just a friend from the road."

"You're back from the forest so soon," the Fae woman, whose name was Blodwen, said. "Did the Mothers accept your offering?"

"The men should be no problem now; I will cut them like a plow. And in the furrows we'll place the seeds of a kingdom that serves the Fae realm's needs."

I tried to pull away, but Oberon was holding me in his powerful grip.

"Tree Man, please!" I said; his fingers were constricting my jaw. "You're hurting me!"

King Oberon ignored me. "Now where is that . . . daughter? Why doesn't she join the dance?"

"She's here, my king," said Blodwen, the worm woman. "But you know her. Shy around our people yet." She glanced over his shoulder at a leafy canopy covering two trees. "Still she asks the wizard for forgiveness."

My ears perked, and I tried to free myself from Oberon's grip.

"Come out here . . . daughter. Hug your father!" Oberon

called, and a flash of anger passed over his face. "Quench my thirsting heart like water!"

The flaps of the canopy parted, and a familiar figure stood in the shadows. She ran through the grass and jumped at King Oberon. He caught her with one hand and held me with the other.

"My brave girl!"

"Father!"

I peered up at the girl, whose eyes were closed, tears leaking from the corners. After a moment she took a breath and opened her lids.

Morgana looked at me in disbelief.

19

You Again

MORGANA'S EYES STAYED WITH ME. HER NOSE WAS BURIED IN Oberon's shoulder, and her eyelids fluttered.

King Oberon whispered in her ear, "My brave little sorceress. You have proved a great success."

"Nosewise?" she said, dropping down to the grass. I flinched.

"Here's your little dog I found," Oberon said, gripping me tighter. "Wandering on the wooded ground."

She looked at Oberon. "You said the riders didn't find—"

"They didn't."

"I'm so happy." Morgana wrapped me in a tight embrace. Oberon released his hand, and I could breathe again.

"Is Merlin here?" I said, my eyes flicking between the incredible sights: Oberon, the Fae dancers, and Morgana embracing me. Her scent was different than I remembered, as if the Fae realm had bent it somehow.

"How did you get here?" she asked, pulling back. Her hands were still on my shoulders, but her grip wasn't tight.

"Followed my nose."

She smiled through wet eyes. "My Asteria," she said, glancing down at my chest. "I thought it was lost."

"I took it with me . . . when I escaped the house."

"Oh, Nosewise. I'm sure you were scared. We have a lot to explain." She clutched my shoulders more tightly now. "But I'm so happy you're alive."

"Merlin?" I said again.

"Oh, he's fine!" Morgana answered, nodding quickly. "He's his stubborn self, but . . . he's all right."

I sniffed Morgana and realized what was different about smells in the Fae. They were all murkier and darker here, and that's why I hadn't been able to recognize them. But now that I'd sensed Morgana's Otherworld scent, I knew what adjustments to make in my Mind's Nose. I considered Oberon's smell again and realized his scent was the same as Lord Destrian's.

Oberon glanced down at me and seemed to sense my recognition. He blinked, and his pointy blue face transformed into a human one. Lord Destrian was looking right at me. I'd never seen illusion magic transform a face that way before, but there was Lord Destrian, smiling and nodding.

I barked and startled Morgana. "Nosewise!" she cried,

but I wrenched out of her grip. Strange Fae bodies danced around bonfires, and glowing trees swayed around me.

I bolted toward the center of the camp, dropped my nose to the grass, and ran zigzag patterns.

Then I caught it: Merlin's shifted scent. Blodwen was in the corner of my eye, but I took off with great speed. "Get him!" the worm woman screamed.

The Otherworld went by in a blur. No one could outrun a dog, not even Oberon. Disturbing shapes broke away from the fires and pursued me, but I ignored them. Dried leaves cracked beneath my feet and felt hot with magic.

The scent led me to an enormous tree. Its roots undulated out of the ground in waves, and massive branches towered above. Sparkling leaves hung down at eye level and obscured nearly everything behind.

I burst through them and felt sparks where they brushed against my fur. Everything was darker inside the reach of the tree, but my nose found him instantly.

"Nosewise?" Merlin said. The shifted smell of his sweat and hair was strong. I blinked and saw that he was seated on a rock and tied to a root.

"Master! I've found you!"

"My boy, how did . . . ?" Merlin pressed his face against my head and sighed. "A friend. So long since I've seen a friend," he whispered. "But you mustn't be here."

"I'm rescuing you!" I said, and examined his ropes. They were just dry, twisted vines.

"You have Morgana's Asteria. . . ."

"Take it! Use its magic."

Merlin stared at it and swallowed. "There's no escape," he said. His face looked pained. "They have the worm sprites, and there are many of them."

"They're coming now," I said. "I'll do it myself!"

"Nosewise?"

I found my Certainty. *Merlin is a very good master.*

In my Mind's Nose I recalled the scent of a tree outside our home that had been struck by lightning. It was burned, broken, and bubbling over with sap. The sensation of lightning buzzed in my mind, and I released it.

Crack!

A small blast of light and energy scorched the tree root and burned the rope.

"How?" Merlin gasped, pulling the withered rope until it broke.

The spell worked. I'd done magic. But rustling leaves and swooshing air turned my head—I was too late.

I was on the ground, trapped by a throng of Fae. Waxy hands and sharp elbows pinned me. Above, the worm sprites slithered through the air. Merlin yelped. More Fae crowded us in the darkening haze.

"Don't hurt him!"

Morgana pushed through the mob and pulled a twig-nosed woman off my chest. She knocked away a young boy with scratchy fingers and lay over me. I locked eyes with her.

"This is for your own good," she said, and reached around the back of my neck.

"Don't!" I shouted, whipping my head. "Please, let us—Arf! Arf! Woof!"

The magic stone was off my neck. The worm woman appeared beside Morgana and wrapped a dried vine around my throat.

I panted and gasped for air. Morgana stood over me, clutching the silver chain. She begged the Fae, "Be gentle! Please!"

The dim Asteria in her hand dangled, flickered, and faded to blackness.

20

Prisoners at the Feast

THE DARK NIGHT OF THE FAE WAS ABOVE US. WIND WHISTLED through the trees with gentle music. In front of us was an enormous stone slab stacked with strange foods. Heaps of baked flowers were gathered in bowls. Roasted tree nuts nestled between soft-boiled sweet vines and steamed with delectable scents. My mouth watered and I felt guilty. Morgana had warned me not to trust strange men offering food.

Turned out she'd been right.

"We're assured our meal isn't poisoned?" Merlin said with a weary voice.

Oberon laughed. "Why would I poison friends of mine, and with foods on which my children dine?"

We were both tied to a deep-rooted post. All around the rest of the stone table, the Fae folk sat. For stools they used carved logs of wood. Thirty or so Fae sat at our table, the biggest one of the dozen in the grove.

Oberon sat at the head. A bonfire rose behind him and

cast his antlered shadow far across the table. He looked at Merlin with a humble smile.

"Though it seems we work at opposing ends"—Oberon leaned over to Merlin, and his shadow grew smaller—"that does not mean we can't be friends."

"My father doesn't want to hurt you," Morgana said, seated to the left of Oberon, opposite us. "He needs your help for the good of the realm."

"Good?" Merlin said, a dark laugh rising from his belly. "What good could come from this? Imprisoning a man and his dog in the woods."

"Our conflict now is in the past," Oberon said, opening his hands. "You and I have no quarrel still. My daughter's stone is found at last, and you are subject to my will. Therefore we mean you no harm and greet you here most pleasantly. So *please* drop your alarm and join our feast most presently."

I looked around at the Fae. They popped colorful flowers in their mouths and sucked soggy vines through shiny lips. Morgana didn't look anything like them.

"Please, let Nosewise go," Merlin said meekly. "You've no use for him here. I'm who you want."

Morgana flinched and looked at Oberon.

"In time you and he will both be free," Oberon said. "But till then can't you stay with me? I'll give you moss to make your bed and keep the raindrops off your head." He turned his enormous hands upward and faced the rest of the table, his loud voice booming. "I am the king of the faerie realm, who rules the world of oak and elm. And you are guests now, man and beast, at the faeries' summer feast."

The entire table erupted in applause, and the Fae slurped their food noisily. I found it gross, which was a first for me.

"I know of the faerie realm," Merlin said. "And you are no king of it. You are merely prince of the Summer court."

The worm woman swallowed the strand of soggy vine she'd been slurping. "Watch what comes out of your mouth," Blodwen said in her throaty voice, "or your teeth will follow." The worms floated around her, completely ignoring the food.

Merlin's face paled. "Nivian and the Winter court must know what you've done. I have called to them."

"Master Merlin—" Morgana started to say, but the worm woman gave her a hard look. "Wizard Merlin," she corrected herself, "my father wants to help."

"Morgana," Merlin said, "why would a Fae impersonate a human knight and steal me from my home in the woods? Not out of charity, I assure you."

"Why won't you listen to us?"

Merlin's expression turned bitter. "Oberon is a master of illusion. He has fooled his soldiers and peasants into believing he is a man, Lord Destrian. Why he has done this, I do not know."

"He's a good ruler!"

Merlin shook his head. "And he's fooled *you* into thinking he's your father! This he did so you would open the Wall of Trees and he could capture me. To what end, I'm still not sure."

Morgana's face turned flush and she scowled. "I am *half* Fae," she said. "My mother was human; that's why I look the way I do. When she died, I was lost. Father spent ages looking for me."

"Do you really believe that, Morgana?"

"You don't *want* it to be true," she said. "You *want* me to be an orphan! You *want* the world to be a terrible place."

"I want what's best for you, and this is *not* it."

I could trust my nose again, and by scent I knew that Merlin was right. Morgana wasn't any closer to being Fae than I was.

"If that's true," Morgana said, "and they only wanted me to open the wall, then why am I still here? What use is there for me?"

Merlin nodded sadly. "I suspect you are kept as a hostage, though an unwitting one. Oberon knows I care for you, and he may threaten your life to make me do his bidding."

Morgana blanched at that and turned to Oberon. His face was unmoved. He blinked once and turned to Merlin.

"Back in the times of ages old, man was a small and tribal fold," Oberon said as though their conversation hadn't happened. He picked up a cluster of singed flower bulbs and ate them casually. "They kept their distance from us folk of the trees and feared us to various degrees. Then *kings* came to unite the lands and guide their people with warring hands."

"Men have waged no war with the Fae," Merlin said. "King Uther, when he lived, commanded respect for your lands! I was his conduit to your world and kept peace between men and Fae."

Oberon leaned in close, and his eyes showed fiery light. "But years ago, *disappeared* was Uther, king of man, and ever since *chaos* has ruled your troubling clan."

Merlin's mouth grew tense and he nodded.

"A local knight, *Lord Destrian*, invaded my woods," Oberon said, laying his enormous palm on the table. "Chopping them down, uprooting them from the ground, and calling them *goods*. On one of his expeditions, my Fae warriors did he meet, and left *empty* was his noble seat. But he had a son who would have filled his chair and continued the war on my woods and my air. So before word might get back of his untimely demise, I crafted my *Destrian* disguise." Oberon passed his hand over his face and took on the features of a man. Human eyes and skin replaced his Fae appearance, but the two antlers still rose from his head. Then he blinked and was Oberon again. The Fae laughed and whistled their approval.

"I ruled in his stead for many a year, spending some time in his castle and some time here. Many battles have been fought between warlord knights—over land, and men, and *logging rights.*" Oberon raised his thick eyebrows and looked seriously at Merlin. "Someone will unite again the ever-striving tribes of men. And whoever pulls the Sword in the Stone will have the power to rule alone."

"So that's your object," Merlin said darkly. "But it cannot be you, Oberon. I've seen the way you rule in your guise as Lord Destrian. You murder, pillage, and act with no regard for human life." The Fae faces around us grew angry. My heart beat faster. "You must allow the sword to find a worthy king. Only then can peace return."

Oberon huffed through his nose and flicked a flower bulb with his finger. "All men are cruel; all men are fools," he said, cracking a smile of long, sharp teeth. "How could it matter which one of *them* rules?"

"Don't eat me!" a familiar voice shouted in the night.

There was commotion in the trees, and I leapt up, barking. The vines kept me at the post. I growled and struggled with them.

Branches rustled at the edge of the camp. I sniffed the air, but we were upwind. Some Fae stood; others held their breath.

A boy came through the leaves with two large Fae holding him by the arms.

It was Arthur. His face was caked with dirt and his shirt was torn. I yipped and wagged my tail furiously.

"Oh, stars!" Arthur called. "Nosewise, it's you! And Merlin!"

"Who is this?" Blodwen said, standing and letting her worms take to the air. They floated over the table, and Morgana covered her Asteria.

"It's only a boy!" Merlin said, trying to rise to his feet. "He hasn't any magic to fight with."

"I clean chamber pots!" Arthur exclaimed in a panic. "Don't eat me!"

"We're not going to eat you, tenderflesh," said one of the sharp-faced Fae.

"Sorry to disturb, my king," said the other. "We found this one wandering near the portal from Grimmshode."

"Wait!" Oberon called. "Have some manners, friends, at least. Invite the boy to join my feast."

Arthur's eyes went wide, and his face dropped a shade in color. "Please . . . don't eat me!" he said emphatically. "I'm very dirty!"

"The king of the woods bids you join him," the taller Fae hissed in Arthur's ear. They pushed him forward and slammed his chest into the stone table slab. The shorter one tied Arthur's hands to the post.

"Nosewise," Arthur said, shaking. "Glad to see you're well."

Did he come in after me?

"Arthur, isn't it?" Merlin whispered behind me. "What are you doing here?"

"Your dog, Nosewise. He met me in the castle and convinced me to help track you here." Arthur turned to me. "See what being brave gets you?"

"Boy, you are familiar to my eyes," Oberon said in a gentle voice. He leaned toward us, and Arthur struggled to pull away. "Do you serve me in my mortal guise?"

"Um, no, I don't think so, sir . . . Fae," Arthur sputtered. "I, uh, served a lord called Destrian."

"This *is* Lord Destrian," Merlin said flatly. I turned to Arthur and yipped.

"What?" Arthur said, his face twitching. "Destrian? You're a Fae?"

Oberon smiled, and his long teeth showed in the firelight.

Morgana rapped her knuckle on the table to get Arthur's attention. "So you're the one who brought Nosewise here?"

Arthur glanced at her. "They captured you too?"

"They didn't *capture* me. These are my family."

"Family?"

"Morgana," Merlin whispered.

"Oh, the one who betrayed them," Arthur said, glancing between Morgana and me. "I see you got your stone back."

"This is Fae land," Morgana said, bristling. "Show some respect."

"I showed this man respect my whole life," Arthur said. He tugged at the vines that bound him to the post. "I knew Destrian was an evil thing!"

The Fae at the table gasped. My tail wagged wildly, and I think Oberon noticed. Fire burst from his palms and sent black chimneys of smoke into the sky. Fae cowered, and Arthur winced. Morgana ducked her head, and I dropped my tail between my legs.

The fire subsided and ash dusted the table. Oberon took

a deep breath and sighed in a tone that made me shiver. He blinked and returned his gaze to Arthur, Merlin, and me.

"I do not expect any of you to understand. After all, you're from the tribe of man. Merlin, when you deliver the sword, these two will be set free. But since the boy and dog cannot humor me and act as guests at our sacred meal because of how strongly they feel that they are right and I am wrong, then I will sing a different song, and treat them not as honored guests, but as *prisoners* for the rest of their time in my realm. Blodwen, take the boy to the Sacred Elm, and tie him there with the barking one. Let them wait until the light of the sun."

Blodwen stood up; the worm sprites circled her arms. She and two Fae guards removed us from the post, but gripped us tight.

"Don't struggle," Blodwen whispered to me. "Or my sprites will make a meal of you."

"Don't hurt him!" Morgana cried.

Oberon gave her an irritated glance. He turned to Merlin. "Once these prisoners we contain, I will take my human guise again." His face shifted and transformed until Lord Destrian was looking down on us. Arthur went pale. Oberon's voice slowed and lost its poetry. "We shall ride our horses tonight . . . to the lake lands . . . as a human knight would do . . . and meet Lord Destrian's soldiers. Then on . . .

to Avalon. They will witness their lord . . . take the sword . . . triumphant."

"Avalon," Arthur whispered.

"Arthur, keep Nosewise safe," Merlin said, still bound to the post.

"I'll protect him!" Arthur shouted as the worm woman dragged us away. Merlin breathed heavy and hard. He flashed me a pained look, and in his eyes I saw the truth.

I was far from home, and there was no protecting me now.

21

The Light in the Darkness

THEY BOUND US TO ONE OF THE GIANT TREE ROOTS WHERE I'D found Merlin.

"After you went through the faerie ring, I didn't know where to go," Arthur said, tied up beside me. "If I was a coward, I'd head back to the castle and be Destrian's prisoner again."

Arthur spoke in a raspy voice. He sounded half-crazed from exhaustion.

"But then I'd be abandoning you." He tried to lean close, but the rope held him back. "So I convinced myself to be a hero and follow you into the Otherworld." Arthur clucked his tongue and nodded. "And here I am, Destrian's prisoner . . . again. So it all worked out."

Leaves crackled in the distance and I perked my ears.

"Someone there?" Arthur said, suddenly panicked.

In between the leaves of the tree I saw a bobbing light.

It was faint and flickering. The leaves parted, and a pair of hands came through, holding a dim Asteria.

It was Morgana. I felt Arthur tense against the vines.

Her eyes were puffy, as if she'd been crying, and her cheeks were flush. She wore the Asteria's silver chain around her neck, but she'd detached the stone, and she was rubbing it with her thumbs.

"Hello, Nosewise."

Morgana shifted the Asteria into one hand. The other she reached out to me, asking whether it was all right to touch. I lowered my head, and she lightly scratched my cheeks.

"Good doggy," she said, trying to smile. "I wanted to say to you before, but I couldn't while Father was near . . ." She swallowed hard and blinked. "I hated the way he treated Merlin. When I opened the wall, he handed me to the soldiers and made me wait with them. He said he would only *talk* to Merlin. And then I heard the fighting. . . ." She closed her mouth and shook her head. "They rushed out once they had him. 'Go back for Nosewise,' I said. But Father wouldn't listen!"

My ears pressed to my head. She was crying again.

"Finally I convinced him to send a rider back to look for you. When they told me the house was burned and you were gone, I thought I'd go mad."

"Had them looking for your stone, too?" Arthur said. "Bet you're glad to have that back."

Morgana glared at him. "Not true," she growled. "And I'm not speaking to you, so I trust you'll shut up."

Morgana seemed angry, but I could tell that underneath she was scared.

"In the end, though, I think Father did the right thing," she said, her voice quivering. "Merlin would never have agreed to come on his own. And Father needs him for the good of the realm. Once he has the Sword in the Stone, he can rule as Destrian and be a good king. That's what the land needs, someone wise and kind—"

"Are you insane?" Arthur interrupted her. "*King* Destrian? He lets his people starve and chains them—"

"You don't know what you're talking about."

"I lived with the brute. I saw what he—"

"You know nothing of my father!"

"Your father? Ha!" Arthur shouted. "Are you a monster too? Under that—what's it called, Nosewise? A glamour!"

Morgana's Asteria flashed suddenly, and flames leapt up from her hand. She shrieked and dropped the burning Asteria in the glowing grass.

"No, where'd it go? Where did it go?" Morgana whispered, panicked. She patted the fallen leaves with her hands. I felt something round and hard near my foot.

The Asteria.

I dropped into my Mind's Nose quickly and made a hasty Certainty.

The Asteria flashed once.

"There!" Morgana gasped, and she grabbed it from under my paw. "My magic," she cooed.

Arthur shot me a surprised look, and I whined, intentionally not meeting his eye.

Morgana lifted her gaze to me. "It's been acting strange since I've had it back. I can't get it to work the way I want. And when I don't expect it, bad things happen. Did you break it? It won't even glow for me unless I'm touching it."

I cried a little through my nose.

"Right," she said, smiling nervously. "Can't talk without it. I wish I could just . . ." She moved her hand like she might extend the stone to me. My ears perked, and I felt the hairs rise on my neck.

"But I shouldn't. That's how this all started, in a way. Father said when he saw you with the Asteria, he knew I was ready to act as my own wizard. That I didn't need Merlin's permission to do what was right."

Her voice was tinged with regret.

"I did my part for the good of the realm," she said, trying to convince herself. "Everyone will see."

"Maybe you'd rather let us go?" Arthur said cautiously.

"What? You both are safe here. My people will protect you."

"Your *people* are a bunch of—" Arthur started some

insult, but I shut him up with a bark. Morgana was upset enough.

She'd been horribly deceived by Oberon, just as I'd been. She wanted to be more than an orphan. She wanted a history she could be proud of. Her life before Merlin had been bad just like mine, but for her, unlike me, life with Merlin hadn't been enough.

I stretched my neck to lick her hands. She cupped the Asteria in her left palm and pulled it away, but let me lick her right.

"Sweet boy," she said. "I've brought you a present." She removed her silver necklace and slid it over my snout. The familiar feeling of the links between my fur was comforting, but without the magic stone, it was distressingly light.

"It's no use to me anymore," she said with a smile. "And it looks so good on you. Take it as a promise that when all this is done, things will go back to the way they were. I'll teach you again. And we'll live together here—Merlin, too."

She kissed me on the snout, and I wagged my tail even though I knew things could never go back.

"We're leaving for Avalon now," she said, standing up. "But they'll bring you something good to eat in the morning." She turned away, blocking the Asteria's light from us. The leaves rustled and she disappeared.

* * *

"Nosewise," Arthur whispered. "Is she gone?"

I had my ears perked, wondering that myself.

I shook the rotted ropes off my body. Arthur did the same, tugging on them until they snapped. "Did you do this?" he asked, holding a length of blackened rope.

When Morgana's Asteria had been under my foot, I'd felt its power and thought of a Certainty.

I won't let them hurt Merlin.

In my Mind's Nose I'd smelled rot. Fire would have been hard to control and Morgana would have noticed. But decay happened more slowly.

"Hey, what happened to my shirt?" Arthur said, tugging on his sleeve—it crumbled off his arm. I supposed it had gotten caught up in the spell. The root of the Sacred Elm was rotting too. The Fae wouldn't like that very much.

I whined at Arthur and bade him follow me through the curtain of leaves. I felt them falling apart on my back as I walked by. We really had to get out of there.

"Where are you going?" Arthur said, grabbing hold of my tail. "The faerie ring to Grimmshode is that way!"

That wasn't the ring I was looking for. During our walk, Oberon had told me that the faerie rings in the Fae realm were linked to portals in our world that were hundreds of miles apart. I thought Oberon had come here as a shortcut to wherever he was going. We had to find the ring they'd just taken Merlin through.

Of course I couldn't tell Arthur this, because I didn't have a voice. So I grumped at him.

"You've got the nose," Arthur said, raising his hands. "Lead the way."

I followed Morgana's trail from where we'd been tied up. It was leading toward the camp.

"Sure it's this way?" Arthur said, crawling through the grass. "If they catch us again, we're not getting home."

I flattened my ears and kept on the scent. The Fae were dancing again. They weren't thinking about intruders.

The trail led to a dark clearing with a dying fire at the edge of camp. Morgana, Merlin, and Oberon had all just been here, along with three horses.

"Nosewise, why are we stopping?" Arthur whispered. I saw that he was dragging himself through the grass like a snake. My tail wagged.

"You think it's funny? I'm ten feet tall compared to you—they're going to spot me first." Arthur popped his head up and scanned the clearing.

There was a circle of dimly glowing mushrooms, all shapes and sizes. A faerie ring.

"Are you sure that's the right one?" Arthur whispered. I crawled out in front of him. I was sure. Their scents were all over it.

We crawled into it, and again I felt the sensation of spiderwebs closing my eyes and pressing my ears. We seemed to squeeze through a soft mound of earth, and then it was daylight again.

Arthur tried to balance but fell on the grass. He pressed his face into it and sighed. "Real grass. It isn't glowing. How wonderful is that?"

We were in an overgrown prairie, which was good, because the long grass helped protect the scents.

"Wait a minute," Arthur said. "This isn't Grimmshode." The landscape was very different. There were hills everywhere and hardly any trees. "Where did it take us?" Arthur asked.

I hated not having the Asteria. I'd gotten used to speaking my mind.

"Did you take us to the Lake Lands?" Arthur asked. I cocked my head, not knowing what he meant. "Near Avalon!" Arthur shouted. "Is this where Oberon went?"

I wagged my tail wildly and pointed down the trail I'd found.

"North. Of course, they went north!" Arthur said, looking very upset. "You followed them! Why didn't you take us home?"

I yelped defensively. I wasn't going to abandon Merlin!

"And we can't go back in there," Arthur said, pointing to the faerie ring. "We'll be caught. They'll soon know we escaped—they'll be coming out after us."

I barked forcefully.

"You want to find Merlin. All right. You haven't given us much choice."

I sensed Arthur was scared. But I also knew he was brave. *He came into the Otherworld after me, even though he didn't have to.*

"If Destrian gets the sword, he'll be king," Arthur said, talking more to himself than me. "We escaped his castle and his weird Fae world. But if he becomes king, there'll be nowhere to run."

I didn't understand what he meant about the sword or about Oberon becoming king, but he looked like he was ready to go my way.

"All right," Arthur said. "But I don't know how far it is to Avalon. I've never been in this part of the country . . . never been anywhere, really."

I sniffed the ground and wiggled my butt.

"Follow your nose, yes," said Arthur. "But it could be far, and they've got horses. So we're chasing someone who's faster than us. And we're bound to be pursued by the Fae once they find we've escaped," Arthur sighed. "Then our only chance is—"

I barked excitedly and charged forward down the scent trail.

"Yes, that's what I meant," Arthur said, taking the rear. "Run!"

PART IV

2 2

❧

No Such Thing as a Free Lunch

IT RAINED. A LITTLE AT FIRST, AND THEN A LOT.

And we ran in the rain for hours. Early morning to late afternoon, we trekked through mud and puddles. The scent trail was hard to keep, and we both got soaked and chilled to the bone.

But at the end of a long day's travel, we arrived at the shore of an enormous lake. I'd never seen anything like it. The lake was so big, it stretched past the horizon.

We wandered into a town on the waterfront and walked up to the biggest building. "I think it's a tavern!" Arthur said, shielding his eyes from the rain and peering at a creaking sign. There were two shapes carved into the wood: a sword and a hand.

Arthur shivered and yanked open the door. I tried to scurry in between his legs, but he clamped his knees against my sides. "I don't know if dogs are allowed."

I whined. There were several dozen people gathered inside. They were warm and dry and feasting on morsels. I smelled mutton, pork, and warm crusts of bread.

Food!

"Barman, excuse me!" Arthur shouted over the rain and murmurs of the crowd. "Can I bring in my dog?"

A burly man with long black hair cinched into a ponytail spun around at the bar and smiled. "Dogs, frogs, cogs, and logs," he said in a cheery voice. "All are welcome, as long as you can pay."

Arthur's face darkened. "Right," he mumbled to himself. "Pay."

His knees relaxed, and I scampered to a nearby table, stacked high with food. I jumped on the bench and buried my face in a juicy pork loin.

"Hey!" shouted a ruddy-nosed woman, who smacked me across the mouth. "Get your muddy dog out of here!"

"Not trained yet!" Arthur grabbed my chain, but I struggled against him for the pork.

"Come, sit by the bar," the tavern keeper said. "I got a rope; we can tie him up."

Arthur dragged me away from the scrumptious meal. I scraped my nails across the floor. "Please behave," he whispered.

"I'd invite you to dry yourselves, but the fire's a bit crowded," the tavern keeper said, gesturing to the back wall. The hearthstone was packed with a dozen soggy travelers. Above them hung hundreds of clay blocks with handprints pressed into them. "Really came on sudden, didn't it?"

I put my paws on the bar and barked.

"Sorry about my dog," Arthur said. He put a cold hand on my snout. "We're just very hungry."

"Don't fret about it. Nothing like a wet dog to give a pub that homey smell." The tavern keeper tied a thin strand of rope to a post and knotted it on my necklace. He whistled through his teeth. "Mighty fancy collar for a dog. Must be something special."

"You don't know the half of it," Arthur said wearily.

The tavern keeper laughed. "I can feed you, but I got to ask that you pay up front. We've had a problem with dine-and-dashers lately." He winked at Arthur. "Not you, of course. Got a silver chain on your dog."

I wagged my tail and Arthur smiled awkwardly. "About payment . . ."

The barman, who was setting down plates and glasses, stopped. "No money?"

"This was an unexpected trip and . . . that's another story. Could we work for you in trade? Dishwashing, maybe?"

The barman looked at Arthur blankly. "Don't really need dishwashers. Half the starving folks in the county want to wash dishes for food. But if no one pays for meals, I've got no dirty dishes."

There were dark circles under Arthur's eyes, and his teeth were chattering. He sighed and rubbed his arms.

"Hate to turn you away," said the man behind the bar. "But if I opened a hand to everyone in need, I'd be the one begging."

I glanced around the tavern. Every bench and stone held someone nursing an ale and a leg of chicken. It made my tummy rumble. *They can't turn us away,* I thought. *I want food!*

I turned to Arthur and saw a wild look in his eyes. He was mouthing something.

"What was that?" the tavern keeper asked.

"Perhaps my dog can do a trick for you? In the form of payment. He knows some magic."

Behind us, eavesdropping patrons turned in their chairs. The barman leaned close.

"He knows what?" he said gruffly.

What is he doing?

"Uh—magic?" Arthur answered uncertainly. "He's a wizard dog. Or a *wizard's* dog," he corrected himself. "He's both, actually."

The barman blinked, then cracked a smile. He looked at me and laughed. The nearby diners joined in, chuckling and jostling each other.

"He can't do magic at the moment," Arthur said among the ruckus. "He lost his magic stone."

"Magic stone!" someone behind us said. "Somebody help the dog find his magic stone!"

I turned to the man and woofed. It's not nice to make fun of someone who's lost something.

"Oh, he didn't like that," said the woman beside him.

"There, there, boy," the barkeep said, ruffling my wet fur

and taking a pot of hot cider from under the bar. He poured two sweet-smelling bowls for Arthur and me. "These are on the house," he said, wiping a tear out of his eye. "For the laugh."

Arthur picked up the bowl with shaking hands and downed it in one long gulp. I leaned over and lapped mine up. It was warm and smooth and hit all the right spots.

"I've seen him do it, you know," Arthur grumbled. "I'm not crazy."

"You know what," the barkeep said, crouching down to my level. He scratched my ears and ran his hand down the fur of my neck, pinching the silver chain between his fingers. "This is as good as money, right here."

After much talk, the barman snipped a single link off my silver chain and pocketed it; the rest he fastened back on my neck. Soon a young girl came by the bar with a heavy tray.

"All right, we've got the Traveler's Feast for the boy with the magic dog." She set down a ceramic plate heavy with pork chops, fried peas and carrots, half a loaf of bread, cubed cheeses, and a spoonful of mashed potatoes. She smiled at Arthur. "And for the wizard dog himself," the girl went on, "the Sheepdog's Dream." She dropped a plate piled high with mutton steaks.

"Guinevere," the barkeep said, "don't tease the guests!"

"Who's teasing?" asked the girl. She was about Arthur's age and smelled like fresh milk. She elbowed Arthur and said, "I believe in your wizard dog." She suppressed a tiny laugh. "When I was little, I had a rabbit that saw the future!"

The patrons behind us laughed, and Arthur blinked rapidly.

"To the tables, Guinevere!" the barkeep ordered. She picked up a pitcher of beer he offered and went. "Excuse my daughter," he said. "And I bid you welcome to the Sword and the Hand. Please, enjoy your meal."

Arthur nodded and tucked into his plate. I savaged my mutton steaks two at a time. *The barkeep gave us this for one link of a chain? How stupid!*

Once we'd eaten and drunk our fill, Arthur was feeling more himself.

"You know, I'm not crazy," Arthur said to the serving girl when she came back to the bar.

"That right? I could have sworn you announced your dog was a wizard!"

Arthur opened his mouth to say something, but glanced back at me. "That was the hunger talking," he finally said. "He's not a magic dog."

I glared at him.

"That's a shame," said Guinevere. "And here I thought you were something special." She took another pitcher of beer and served the other patrons.

"Don't let her get to you," the barman said. "Guinevere only teases the ones she likes."

"What? You think I . . . no!" Arthur said.

"I'm only joking, boy!" The barman poked Arthur playfully. "My name is Leodegrance, but my friends are a bunch of drunk people"—he gestured to the patrons—"so they just call me Leody. You can too."

"Um . . . hello, Leody," Arthur said, crossing and recrossing his arms in an attempt to look comfortable.

"Can I ask what you and your well-jeweled dog are doing in the Lake Lands? I'm not just proprietor of the Sword and the Hand tavern, I'm mayor of this town, so I like to know who's visiting."

"Well," Arthur whispered, looking over his shoulder, "we're heading to Avalon."

"To Avalon!" Guinevere said, popping up from some unseen place and sidling up to the bar. "Do you intend to have your magic dog pull the sword from the stone?"

Arthur's face flushed and he turned to her. "No, I'm n-not going to have my dog do it," he sputtered. "We're going to Avalon because . . . well, it isn't your business, is it?"

"Guinevere!" Leody thundered so everyone could hear. "Isn't it obvious? This boy's going to try his hand at taking Excalibur from the stone. Show some respect! This could be your future king we're talking to!"

The bar quieted for a moment. Leody's huge hands stayed in the air and Guinevere's eyes were wide.

Then everyone broke into laughter.

Arthur stewed silently as they guffawed. He made a face and took a swig of his cider. I stared at the laughing patrons. If only I had my Asteria, I'd show them we were nothing to joke about.

I put my forepaws on the bar and barked in Leody's laughing face. "Woof!"

He closed one eye and peered at me with the other. Then I turned to Guinevere and barked at her as well.

"Only teasing, boy," Leody said, patting my neck. "We've had some pretty impressive knights waltz in here the last ten years—all with an eye on taking the sword. But each has come back empty-handed." He gestured to the walls filled top to bottom with hand impressions in clay. "We like to get one of those made before someone takes the trip in case they do come back triumphant. But it's really become a wall of shame."

"Well, I'm sorry to disappoint you," Arthur said, trying to avoid Guinevere, who was leaning against the bar and staring at him, "but I'm not trying to pull the sword. I have other business there."

"Other business in Avalon?" Guinevere said. She tried to catch Arthur's eye, but he stared at the bottom of his cider glass. "You know that no one lives there. There's nothing to do in Avalon but seek the sword and maybe die if you're not lucky."

"My dog and I have business there, and that's all you

need to know," Arthur said, accidentally making eye contact. He twitched, and I watched his face flush again. This girl had a strange effect on him.

"You're right," Leody said from behind the bar. "And if you want a ferry to Avalon, I'll have one of my men take you tomorrow if the weather gets better. What do you say to two links of that chain for the ride?"

"I say fine," Arthur answered. "But we should leave first thing in the morning."

"You can't go sailing if it's still raining," Guinevere said, touching Arthur's arm. He tensed and pulled it closer to his chest.

"My ferrymen won't go out in this weather," Leody said seriously. "Rain will fill your boat and you'll be bailing the whole way." He turned to Guinevere. "I feel terrible for that big knight that set off this morning. He and his party are probably half drowned by now."

My ears perked up at that. I grumped at Arthur and barked.

"What's the matter with your d—"

"Did you say a big knight?" Arthur interrupted.

"Yeah," Leody answered. "Lord Destrian, wasn't it? Got the hands right here," he said, pulling from under the bar a clay block with two enormous handprints in it. "But he wouldn't take his gauntlets off for the pressing, or his helmet, either. I thought that was strange."

"Was there an old man with him?" Arthur asked, untying me. I scurried across the room, smelling the floors, walls, and benches. At the far corner of the tavern my nose lit up. Merlin had been here.

"Yeah, he was sitting there," Guinevere said. "An old man in a heavy cloak and hood. A soldier waved me away when I tried to take his order."

"There were soldiers?"

"About twenty of them," Leody said. "They've been hanging around town for a week. Ran up an incredible bill. Then Destrian arrived with the old man and a little girl and they left for Avalon. Said they were trying the sword."

I ran back, barking.

"Get that dog under control!" shouted one of the patrons.

"The old man is his master," Arthur said. "And Lord Destrian kidnapped him. *That's* why we're going to Avalon."

I jumped up on Guinevere and barked. She held my face and clucked her tongue. "He was all right," she said. "Don't worry."

"We need a boat right now!" Arthur slapped his hand on the bar.

"I told you, no ferryman will take you!" Leody said, flustered.

"Then we'll buy the boat ourselves!" Arthur said, unhooking my silver necklace. "This enough?"

Leody looked uneasy. "In good conscience, I couldn't . . ."

"Listen to me—Lord Destrian's an evil man. He'll hurt our friend, maybe kill him. We've got to get there before it's too late."

Pride welled up in me, seeing Arthur like this. He was fighting for what was right, but he did keep glancing at the girl. She seemed to give him courage.

"All right," Leody said, taking hold of the silver necklace. "In truth, this is worth a bit less than a boat, but I'll hang on to it. If you bring my vessel back in one piece, we'll work out fair payment." He turned to his daughter. "Guinevere, take them out and show them the little white sloop. That should be easier to maneuver in the rain."

She nodded, and Arthur got up to follow her.

"Wait!" Leody said, grabbing hold of Arthur's arm. "I never let someone leave for Avalon without pressing one of these." He pulled out a heavy cloth sack and a wooden frame. He dropped the frame on the bar and mashed wet clay into it from the sack. "Never know what can happen in a place like Avalon."

Arthur smiled and pushed his hand into the clay. It came away and left an impression. The barkeep pulled out a small knife and asked, "How should I inscribe it?"

"Um . . . Arthur," Arthur answered. "That's all the name I've got." The barman nodded and carved letters in the clay.

I jumped up, barked, and nudged Leody aside to press my own paw in. When I lifted it, I saw that my pads had made a perfect impression, with little holes where my nails had been.

"Better make that Arthur and *Nosewise*," Arthur said.

23

The Sailor's Dog

"ARE YOU REALLY GOING AFTER A KNIGHT AND SOLDIERS?" Guinevere asked. Outside, the sky was darkly overcast and rain came down in a steady pour. We were walking across the wooden docks that reached into the lake behind the tavern. There were a half-dozen boats tied up, some large and flat and a few tall ones with enormous masts. They were all covered by thick tarps that kept out the water.

"They've got our friend," Arthur said over the sound of rain beating the lake. Just a few minutes outside and we all were soaked. Guinevere seemed completely at home in it.

"But you can't fight soldiers—you're a boy and a dog," Guinevere said, leading us to the back of the dock. There was a small boat hidden in the others' shadows. It was narrow and low to the water, with a single mast about as tall as two men. Guinevere untied the knots that held its protective tarp in place. "Is he going to use his magic powers?" Guinevere said, shaking her head at me. She undid the last knot and pulled at the tarp until the deck was open to the rain. "Crazy people have died traveling to Avalon before, and that's their right. But I don't like to see them take an innocent with them."

I whined and put my forepaws on the side of the boat next to Guinevere. I locked eyes with her and gave a mournful bark. I wished I had my voice.

"He is a smart one. It's almost like . . ."

"He understood you, yes," Arthur said, helping her with the last corner of the tarp. "He's not an ordinary dog."

Guinevere looked at me a minute more and nodded. "You ever sail a boat before?" she asked, and Arthur shrugged. Guinevere looked up at the rain. "Well, it's a fine day to test your luck," she said, hopping over the side of the boat. "I'll give you the short version."

I jumped on too and tried to follow what Guinevere said about the ropes and pulleys that worked the sail. But mostly I focused on not throwing up. Even docked, the boat never stopped rocking. For the first time in my life, I wished I'd eaten less.

"With rain like this, you're going to need to bail out the boat with your pail every half hour. And if the Lady gets angry and sends us any more—well, then you'll never stop bailing."

"The Lady?"

"The Lady of the Lake," Guinevere answered. "The Lady of Avalon. Nivian, the water walker."

"Heh," Arthur laughed uncomfortably. "You've seen this 'water walker'? You talk like you know her."

Guinevere considered Arthur seriously. "You don't need to see a person in the flesh to know them. You see what they do. Nothing happens on this lake that Nivian doesn't want to happen. And by the looks of the sky, she doesn't want anyone coming to her island today."

"Well, if we see her, I'll tell her sorry for intruding," Arthur said, picking up a wooden pole.

Something about this Nivian sounded familiar to me, but I didn't remember why.

"Oh, by the Lady!" Guinevere cursed and pointed down at Arthur's feet. "You're not going to Avalon like that, are you?"

Arthur looked down. "What, barefoot?" Arthur said, wiggling his toes.

"You can't go to Avalon without shoes."

"I haven't needed them yet."

"No." Guinevere made an irritated face. "In Avalon, there's snow on the ground all year. You won't last a minute like that."

"But it's summertime," Arthur said. I perked my ears at Guinevere. Was she teasing us?

"It's Avalon," she said simply. "And you need a pair of shoes." She dropped down on the deck of the boat, which was already filling with water, and yanked at the heels of her boots. "Come on!" she shouted as she struggled with them. "The cursed rain's shrunk them!"

"I'm not going to fit in those; they're girls' shoes!"

"You'll fit," Guinevere said, nodding her head vigorously. Finally she popped off the right one and tossed it at Arthur.

Arthur picked the boot out of the rainy bottom of the boat and sat on the side bench. "There's no way these are going to f—"

The boot slipped onto Arthur's foot, snug as a glove. I wagged my tail as Guinevere tossed him the other one.

"Remember what I said about the wind," she said, stepping out of the boat. "If it gets too strong, drop the sea anchor." She held up a cone-shaped piece of heavy cloth that was attached to the back of the boat with a rope. "It'll slow you down and keep you crosswise with the waves." She threw it in a box by the mast and unhooked the chain mooring the boat to the dock. I felt the deck shift beneath my feet and struggled to keep my balance. "Don't raise the sails until you've got a good wind!" she said, kicking the boat away with her bare foot.

We drifted into the lake.

Arthur dropped a long pole in the water and pushed us farther out. Rain had already filled the bottom of the boat to my toenails.

"And don't forget to keep bailing!" Guinevere called from the dock, the rain making her voice harder and harder to hear. "Five inches on the bottom is your limit!"

"I won't forget!"

"I hope you don't die!" Guinevere shouted, and her voice was just barely audible. "You better bring back my boots!"

"Thank you, we won't! Not going to die, that is! I'll bring back the boots!" Arthur swallowed and looked at me. "Hopefully, we'll live."

I stood on the back of the boat and barked goodbye.

It was miserably wet. The deck of the boat filled with water, and every few minutes Arthur had to take a break from rowing to bail with a little bucket. My paw pads and hind-quarters itched from sitting in the wet, and I jumped on a bench that was built into the side. But the higher I was on the boat, the more the rocking made me sick.

Arthur had the worst of it. His hair dripped water into his eyes, and he had to row the boat. I wished I could do something to help.

The sun set behind the storm clouds, and the wind picked up. Arthur threw the paddle on the deck and sat on the wet floor.

"Wind seems good enough," he said. "Let's try the sail."

He picked at knots and unfolded cloth with wet, slippery hands. He mumbled to himself as he worked, trying to remember what Guinevere had told him. He pulled hard against a scratchy rope and raised the sail to the top of the mast.

Instantly the sail filled up, big and wide. The boat lurched and cut through the rippling water. I jumped on the back bench and watched our wake cut through tiny waves.

"We're moving!" Arthur shouted, throwing his hands to the rain. My tail wagged and cast off drops of water.

"Take us to Avalon!"

24

Caught Sleeping in the Storm

IN MY DREAMS I WAS SHIVERING. I'D ROLLED IN A PILE OF DEER dung outside our house, and Merlin was forcing me to take a bath. The water was cold, and my face was pressed down in it. I couldn't breathe.

I woke up with my snout in a pool of chilly water. My lungs felt wet, like I was drowning from the inside out. The boat was flooded so high that it reached my belly when I stood.

Arthur was asleep on the front bench. I barked, and his eyes shot open. "No! Curse it!"

A great wave of black water crashed over the side of the boat, further flooding the deck. "I've got to bail!" Arthur shouted. He waded to the bucket, which was floating around the back of the boat. The waves were bigger than before; they were tossing us.

We'd both fallen asleep. The boat was running dangerously low to the lake. I put my paws on the side and saw us tip into the water's surface.

Arthur was tossing buckets of water overboard. I tried to flick some out with my snout, but it just ran off me. *A spell of shock would be so useful now.*

Lightning illuminated the lake, and I saw white boulders that seemed to float in the water.

Then the thunder came. My ears rumbled and my feet shook at the sound. I whined and ran across the boat to Arthur.

Behind me, I heard the mast creak as the sail strained in the wind. The boat was speeding over the waves and bouncing us.

A bolt of lightning struck the lake, and boiling water exploded upward. The thunder came with it, and I thought of the lightning storms outside the house in the woods. I would dive beneath the bed for comfort, and at the end of it all, Merlin would come fish me out.

I wished there were a bed I could hide under now.

Crack! The entire boat quaked as a dark object collided with the left side. Water streamed off the top of it onto the boat. "Rocks?" Arthur said, baffled. He ran to the big wooden lever at the back of the boat and pulled it hard.

We lurched to the right, but only slightly. More dark objects collided with the boat, jostling and shaking it. I ran to the front. Lightning flashed again, revealing a sea of floating white boulders.

I barked a warning to Arthur.

"Ice rocks?" he shouted. "Give me the sea anchor! We're going too fast!"

His voice barely broke over the roar of the waves, but I heard him. I ran across the rapidly flooding deck and threw open the small wooden box with my nose.

We never should have come, I thought in a flash.

I bit down on the thick cone of cloth and ran to the back of the boat as the corded rope trailed behind.

"Give it here!" Arthur commanded, taking his hand off the lever and snatching it from me. The lever swung to the opposite direction, and Arthur dropped the sea anchor to grab it. "Throw it!" he shouted.

I picked up the cloth cone and put my forepaws on the back of the boat. A wave rocked us and my paws slipped. I was falling over!

The sea anchor dropped into the water, and I followed it. Then a sharp pain caught my tail, and I hung, suspended. My chest and face were in the churning water, but Arthur was hauling me up by my hind legs. I crumpled into the flooded boat, which wasn't much drier than the lake, and Arthur took the lever again.

The boat jerked as though it had caught something. The whole ship wiggled, and then straightened and slowed. The sea anchor was working. Arthur pulled hard on the lever, and we turned to the right, passing by a mass of floating icy rocks.

"We've slowed down!" Arthur shouted. Our boat cut across waves but they didn't tip us. "I think it's under control!"

I wished we could see better. It was so dark.

My wish was answered a hundredfold when a bolt of

lightning lit up the sky. The lake was crowded with sharp and craggy ice rocks. Arthur screamed, and I yipped.

The lightning bolt had hit our mast. It split in two and was spewing flames.

I felt Arthur push me as the mast tipped toward us and fell.

After that, there was nothing.

25

Rude Awakening

I HEARD GENTLE SPLASHING.

My eyes cracked open, and the glassy lake twinkled sunlight at me. I was shivering.

There was a craggy white block of ice under me. It was bobbing slightly.

I scanned the horizon and whined. The sun rose through thin clouds and reflected off floating white rocks.

Where is Arthur?

The boat, I remembered, had been tossed in the storm. Lightning had struck the mast. There was a plank of wood knocking against the ice block beneath me. It smelled like it came from the boat.

My eye hurt and my cheek was swollen. It was hard to breathe through my nose.

Where is Arthur?

I barked for him through a sore throat. I howled. I yelped.

I sniffed the air and smelled seabirds, fish, and foam. A human smell was traveling on the wind.

I jumped in the water and swam toward it.

I coughed and tried to keep my snout above the surface. The water was cold and the lake very big.

Then I neared a wooden raft. My eyes were bleary, but I recognized a human shape on it. I scrambled to get my front legs onto the wreckage. It dipped a few inches but held.

I pulled myself up and collapsed. Arthur was lying there.

I nosed his ear slightly, and his head rolled away from me. His hair was wet, and he felt cold.

I whined and raised myself a little. I licked his neck and yelped to wake him up.

Nothing.

I crawled onto his chest.

He didn't move.

2 6

Water

I stepped on top of Arthur and pushed his face with my nose. His head lolled back and forth limply.

I barked for help. "Woof! Woof!"

The lake was vast and empty. I cried and yipped, but Arthur wouldn't wake. I looked at him and sniffed his neck. He was a boy I'd met in a castle on my way to find Merlin. I'd convinced him to come with me. Now he was dead.

I sat down on the raft and howled. My throat hurt so much, but the pain couldn't match what I felt in my heart.

The sun was shining—and everything was lost.

27

Nivian

THE WOODEN RAFT, WHICH HAD BEEN BOBBING GENTLY ON THE water, grew still.

I smelled seaweed.

Long reeds snaked up from below the boat and curved around the edges. The wind sounded like a flute.

My tail dropped between my legs and I crawled on top of Arthur. What was happening? Thick grass was growing right out of the lake and surrounding us. It got taller and taller and cast shadows over Arthur.

I looked down and saw that the grass was pressing between the wrecked planks of wood. I felt us jerk like we were being lifted in the air.

Crack! The planks broke apart, and Arthur and I rolled onto a thick mass of wet vines and grass. I tried to stand up, but it was hard to balance on the spongelike plants below.

Above me the reeds were climbing higher and higher until they blocked the rising sun. The light that came through them was strange. The reeds were twisting and bending themselves into the rough shape of a woman.

It reminded me of the leaf man Oberon had made in the Outdoor Study. I barked at it.

The twisty reeds cracked and thickened and formed their shape in front of the sun, and the wind blew so hard and loud that I had to close my eyes.

When I opened them, the reeds had died down and were relaxing into the lake. The wind was gone, and a woman was standing in front of me.

The sun half shone through her long white hair and thin shawl. Her face glowed like the Fae, and her eyes were set wide and almond-shaped. She bent over me, dripping warm water onto my head.

"Nosewise," she said, "I've been watching you."

I barked loud and crouched over Arthur's body.

Who is she? I thought, and growled low. She was a Fae, and the Fae were *not* my friends.

"Yes, I am Fae," she said, as though she'd heard my thought. "My name is Nivian, Lady of the Lake. Have you heard of me?"

My ears perked at that. Guinevere had mentioned the Lady of the Lake. And hadn't Merlin and Oberon talked about a Nivian?

"I am both," the Lady said; she laughed like a string being plucked on a lute. "I was the master of your master."

The master of my master? I thought, trying to work out what she'd said. It felt like there was a stranger in my head, touching my thoughts with small hands. It was scary.

"Your master, Merlin," she said. "When he was young, he traveled here to my lake. I saw he was wise and took him in."

Merlin's teacher! That's where I'd heard the name before. He talked about her sometimes after dinner, or mumbled her name in his dreams.

"In his dreams?" the lady said with an embarrassed smile. She floated down to the leafy raft and seemed to sit on her knees. If she had knees. Everything below her waist was covered by the long shawl, and vague.

"This is your friend?" she said, looking at Arthur. He was still cold underneath me.

He's hurt, I thought.

"More than hurt," the Lady said. "The water took his life."

I yelped.

"But the water and I are friends," she said, brushing the wet hair out of his face with her fingers. "I will ask the water to give it back."

My sore, stiff tail wagged. She laid her palms over Arthur's eyes and blew gently between her lips.

Water, I thought, begging, *don't take Arthur away from me*.

His nose gurgled.

Smelly gunk burbled from his mouth and flowed over his cheeks. He gasped for air, and his eyes twitched beneath closed lids. I pushed his chin up with my nose and licked his face. His throat sounded clear and his breathing was slow.

The Lady looked at me, her hands still on Arthur's temples. "The water agreed."

Thank you, I thought. *Thank you.* I licked her hands. She tasted like fish, fresh baths, and seabirds. She stroked my head. Her arms were wet but warm, and I felt a comforting light spread through me. My cramps and aches gently faded.

She held my face in her hands and massaged my ears with her thumbs.

How can you understand me? I thought. *I lost my Asteria.*

"Words are hard and made of the earth," she said, forming a fist and then opening her hand. "I am of the lake."

How do you know my name?

"I see it written upon your face," she said. "Your name and deeds are clear to me."

I crossed my eyes, trying to look at my nose. *Written on my face?*

The Lady laughed. "Most mortals tell their stories with their eyes—dogs especially." She tilted her head, looking deep into me. "You have love for Merlin. And this boy. Arthur is his name?"

I gave a little yip.

"And you feel pain," she said. "For your girl, Morgana. My brother has hurt you both."

My tail stiffened. *Your brother?*

"Oberon," she said, letting go of my face.

I jumped away from her and barked. Panic filled my chest and I stood over Arthur. I'd trusted a Fae once before.

You're Oberon's sister?

The Lady smiled. "He hasn't been kind to you, I know."

Please leave us, I begged. *Thank you for helping Arthur, but go!*

"He's my brother, and I must love him," she said. "But he's hurt me too."

How could he hurt you?

"What he's done to Merlin," she said. "What he's going to do."

What is he going to do? I thought. *Everyone seems to understand but me!*

"For a thousand years my brother and I have watched the human world, never taking part. But Oberon has grown tired of staying in his—"

Wait, I thought, interrupting. *You're a thousand years old?*

She laughed. "Much older than that. We Fae don't age as you mortals do." The Lady crept beside me and stroked my head. "The passage of time makes you frail. That's why the Fae must protect the mortal world."

That's not what Oberon thinks. I looked down at Arthur. He was sound asleep.

"He believes humans must be dominated; that is how he would protect them." Nivian's voice had music in it, just like her brother's, though she didn't speak in rhyme. Instead she half sang her words.

Do you think that? I asked.

"No," Nivian said with powerful finality. There was magic in her voice, and I could feel it working its way inside me. "There is good in mortals, which is why I give them power to rule themselves."

How do you do that?

"I give them the Sword in the Stone," she said with a smile.

My ears perked. I'd heard Merlin and Oberon talking about that before. Something about becoming a king?

"It is a magical sword," Nivian said, cradling something in her hands. "One of great power."

Maybe my eyes were playing tricks on me, but I swore that I could see it there. The hilt was gold and the blade shining silver. "Excalibur, the sword of power, is as old as the world. When it came into my possession, I bound it in stone," said Nivian. She stuck the illusion of the sword into the spongy plants and it stayed there. "Only a worthy soul who loves man and would never do him harm might take it." I pushed my nose through the illusion, and it disappeared.

Is it magic?

"Of a kind; it grants its wielder strength and skill. For hundreds of years I've released the sword to worthy leaders and called it back after their deaths. The human world has come to see anyone wielding Excalibur as a rightful king or queen."

Is that why Oberon wants it? I thought. *He pretends to be a human and dresses like a knight.*

"Yes," said the Lady of the Lake, and a deep furrow dug in her brow. "My brother's ridiculous disguise, Lord Destrian. He embarrasses me."

Why did he take Merlin? I asked. *Is he the worthy soul?*

Nivian smiled and wrapped her long arm around me. "Merlin is very good," she said. "But like most humans, he has vanity in him. He wields his power wisely, but—"

Magic is for those with the wisdom to wield it!

The Lady laughed. "I taught him that. I'm glad he's still repeating it. Merlin is wise enough for the power he wields. But there is something greater than wisdom."

What's that?

"Goodness," she answered. She glanced at Arthur and then looked back at me. "Merlin is not the worthy soul."

Then why did Oberon take him?

"Do you know the difference between Summer and Winter magic?"

I thought back to my days in the Outdoor Study, when Morgana gave me lessons.

Summer magic is fast and strong, I recited from memory. *Winter magic lasts a lifetime long.*

"Very good," she said, stroking my fur. "My brother is of the Summer Fae. He's a master of illusion, but his power pales compared to mine. I am Winter Fae. My brother makes icicles—I create glaciers. The sword is bound with Winter magic, of which my brother knows none."

Did you teach Merlin Winter magic?

"I did. Though now I wish I hadn't. An unworthy soul attempting to pull the sword is like a child trying to lift a boulder. Merlin knows the secrets of my enchantment; he can dislodge the boulder from its place, but it will roll back and crush him. Oberon knows this."

Breaking the spell will kill Merlin? I sprang up and barked.

"That's why I grew that awful storm," the Lady said. "My magic is stronger than my brother's, but slow. I hoped to sink their boat and hold them at my mercy. But Oberon's worm sprites consumed the magic of my storm, giving them clear sailing. They landed last night."

Those worms are scary.

"To a magic user, yes," the Lady answered. "Blodwen has twisted the creatures of the Fae world. Oberon uses the sprites to keep my and Merlin's power in check."

So you can't help him?

"The magic of Winter is strong enough to freeze or boil the waters of this lake. But it takes time. The worm sprites consume my magic too quickly. If they were gone, there might be a chance, but even then, half my strength is tied up in the sword's enchantment."

I looked down at Arthur. His hair was drying in the rising sun. His chest lifted and fell gently. He smelled fresh and clean, like he'd just taken a bath.

He is a worthy soul, I thought. *Arthur is good. He had nothing to gain by helping me in the Otherworld. If he pulled the sword, would that save Merlin?*

The Lady smiled coyly. "You'll need to try to be sure. But yes, maybe the right one is here." She looked down at Arthur and then back up to me. She reached out her hand, and I saw the way it shimmered and glowed like a ripple in the water. I sniffed her fingers and licked her. She laughed.

"There are some who think that magic is beyond simpler creatures. I'm afraid that your master, Merlin, was one of them."

I looked up at her, ashamed.

"But they are wrong," she said. "I haven't had a student in sixty years, not since I met Merlin as a boy and saw he had the Knack. I could teach much to one like you."

But I'm no wizard, I thought. *I couldn't even keep my Asteria.*

"Talent doesn't lie in an Asteria, or in any magical point of focus. It lies within. And you, Nosewise, have a Talented soul."

Unable to control myself, I jumped on Nivian and licked her forearms. She laughed loudly and embraced me.

"And such a Talent needs an instrument to match. I won't send you off defenseless."

The Lady of the Lake set me down on my feet and gestured toward the seaweed beneath her. A twisted tendril rose up and unfurled in the air. A leafy knot at the center grew smaller and smaller as the vine extended itself and finally unwrapped a present.

It was a smooth, clear stone. It glowed with an inner light and chimed in tune with the wind. It was beautiful.

An Asteria for me? I thought. My tail wagged and I barked.

"Not a true Asteria that falls from the sky," the Lady of the Lake said. "But one taken from the sand and glass of this lake, and fashioned just for you." She weaved strands of seaweed into a braided collar and attached it to the stone. I shuddered as it passed over my face.

"You'll need it where you're going."

"To Avalon?" I said aloud. My tail wagged and I smiled broadly. "I can speak again!"

"You can do more than that," the Lady said. "This stone is strong, and on Avalon it will be stronger yet. I've given you the best chance to save our friend."

"Thank you!" I said happily. "But we don't have a boat."

"You don't?"

The weeds beneath us shifted and curled. Walls of vine rose, and a sturdy reed grew up from the center to form a mast. Leaves unfurled and made an organic sail. Wind filled the sail and pressed us forward.

My stomach twisted as the boat slid down the hill of seaweed and crashed into the water. It was buoyant and bouncy and cut a trail through the lake, dodging the floating boulders of ice.

We picked up speed, and Nivian lowered through the bottom of the boat like water through soft ground. She caressed my chin lightly with her hand as she went. "Do good, little dog."

She closed her eyes and descended into the lake. The last I saw of her was her silver-white hair slipping through the vines.

Behind me, I could hear Arthur waking up.

PART V

2 8

The Frozen Island

WE CRUNCHED ONTO THE BEACH. UNDERNEATH THE BOAT, ICE blocks cracked, and slush sprayed onto the deck.

Arthur sat up at the impact. His breath showed in the cold air and his cheeks were flush.

He looked like he had no idea what was going on.

"Arthur! You're awake," I said. "How are you feeling?"

He turned to me, glassy-eyed, and his lip quivered.

"It's Nosewise. You recognize me. We're past the lake—we're on the shore. Look! We've landed on Avalon!"

I barked and turned to the snowy world in front of us. Huge piles of ice made up the edge of the island. Waves crashed into them and sent up cold mist. Rolling white hills and enormous frozen boulders spread into the distance. At the end of it all sat a wide mountain. White snow, black boulders, and tall pines grew into the sky on its rocky slope. I had a feeling we were heading there.

I looked back at Arthur and saw that his eyes were widening. "We've arrived," I whispered.

He gripped the front of the spongy boat and pulled himself forward. Then Arthur dropped to his knees, leaned over the edge, and vomited violently overboard.

We climbed down into the snow, and I noticed that the organic boat was already freezing over.

Arthur rubbed his hands against his arms and shivered.

I did my best to explain to him what had happened, but it was hard. Arthur didn't pay much attention to my tale of the Lady of the Lake, to my new Asteria, or even to the fact he'd been dead (which would have bothered me). He was focused on one thing, and one thing only.

"It's cold! Holy heavens and earth, why is it like this?" Arthur jumped up and down and shouted. He trudged through the snow, shivering and shaking. His lips turned pale and his teeth chattered.

I loved it and couldn't help myself from leaping about. My paws crushed the snow in a satisfying way, and it felt great to rub my face in the drifts. I vaulted through misty piles, arcing in the air and coming down with a *crunch*.

"Arthur, it's so much fun!" I shouted as I ran by him, kicking up little flurries with my tail.

"Nosewise, s-s-s-stop it!" Arthur stammered.

"Don't you want to play?" I asked. "Look where we are! I haven't seen snow since I first came to Merlin's! Are you feeling all right? You were dead before, and that can't be good for you."

"What? Don't say things like that. I was never dead!"

"You were dead," I said. "I saw you. And the Lady told me—"

"Nosewise, I'm freezing cold!"

"This summer's been so hot," I replied. "Don't you think it's nice to be in a place—"

"I don't have a fur coat like you, Nosewise! Look at me!"

I turned to Arthur and realized what he meant. He was wearing a thin shirt with no sleeves (I'd rotted them away in the Fae realm) and short pants. I thought back to the kinds of clothing Merlin and Morgana wore when it was winter at the house in the woods. They liked to tromp around in thick coats with heavy hats and gloves.

"You're not dressed right at all."

"I kn-kn-kn-know that, Nosewise," Arthur said, shivering. "Thank goodness for these b-boots Guinevere lent me." Color rose to his cheeks again, but it was brief.

"I can try and make some fire for you," I said, bounding toward him through the snow.

"Really? That would be very nice."

Arthur held out his shaking hands and I dropped down into my Mind's Nose. I smelled the warm crackling scents of our hearth at the house in the woods and focused on my favorite Certainty.

Pffoom!

Great gusts of flames spewed out of my Asteria in a burning tower. Arthur screamed and leapt into the snowy drift. I yelped and backed away from the heat. My mane at the bottom of my neck was smoldering, and I dropped into the snow.

Then I ran to Arthur. He looked frightened, but he grabbed my shoulders and I helped him up. His whole back was covered in ice, and he knocked it off with frozen hands.

"What was that?" he asked.

"I don't know. I'm sorry. That's more than I've ever done before. When I cut Merlin from the tree, the lightning was small and sharp. That fire was . . ."

"Enormous," Arthur said. "And *warm*. Do it again—but a bit farther away this time."

I concentrated again on the scent of fire and noticed that there was something different about this place. After all, it *was* winter here while summer reigned everywhere else. And Nivian had told me that my new Asteria would be powerful on Avalon.

I didn't know what was happening—but I could feel that it was *something*.

"Brilliant, Nosewise!" Arthur shouted as he held his hands to the fire spouting from my Asteria. Now that the bottom fluffs of my mane had burned away, the magic could pass through me easily. Back at the house, Merlin had said that magic was a swift river and a skilled boatman could go far. It seemed the magic was stronger here and I was riding a powerful wave.

Merlin had said something about drowning, too. But when I thought of that, my fire sputtered out and died.

I must keep my Certainty.

29

The Melted Summer Path

WE TRUDGED ONWARD LIKE THAT FOR SEVERAL HOURS. ARTHUR would shiver and chatter and complain as we walked through the "thigh-high snow," as he called it, and when the cold became too much for him, I would turn around and do some magic.

It was good practice. At first I just blew streams of fire, as that was what came naturally to me. But as I did it over and over (Arthur was *very* cold), I found that I could adjust the shape and size of the spell with my mind. I could make it come out in little fireballs, or as a swirling flame. But I had to be careful to send it away from me or else it burned my chin. I lost a lot of whiskers that way and wished Merlin were near to help me.

But I wasn't having any luck finding his scent trail. Everywhere else I'd been, the motes of hair and skin had sat on the ground or gotten kicked up in the wind. Here, snow and ice locked the scents beneath the falling snow. We were just wandering aimlessly.

"Ouch! Arthur, it's happened again!" I yelped, and flopped on a hard pile of snow.

"Don't bite it!" Arthur commanded, but I was already furiously nibbling between my toe pads.

"It hurts!" I shouted. "I hate it."

"You're going to bite your feet open. Now give it here!" Arthur pushed my head away and got to picking out compacted bits of snow that had wedged between my paws.

I howled. "You're doing it wrong! That hurts! Let me bite it!"

"Nosewise, you're such a baby," Arthur said. "There. You're done."

I stood up on the crusty snow and my feet sank through. My tail wagged. Then I ran again, leaping through it in waves.

"You keep up like that, it's going to happen again!" Arthur shouted behind me.

"But it's just so fun!"

I loved the snow—even if it got caught in my toes, it was worth it just to feel that crunch. *Crunch. Crunch. Crunch.*

Thud.

I shook my head and found myself on the ground. Not snowy ground either, but thick, wet grass. I looked up and saw that I was in something like a snow trench. It was piled up to my shoulders on either side of me. But a grassy path cut right through it.

"Ahh!" Arthur lost his footing on the slippery grass and fell alongside me. He groaned and made to get up, but before he could, he stopped in a hunched position with his hands held out. "What's this?" he said.

"I don't know. The snow is melted here."

"And it's *warm*. The ground is warm, the air is warm . . ." He stood to his full height and gasped. "Cold again!" He crouched and sighed with relief. "It's good down here. But when I get too high—eep!" He stretched his head as far as he dared and dropped back down.

I caught some familiar scents. Merlin, Morgana, Oberon, and a whole host of men in iron and leather. Their trails were all on the ground before me. I looked up the path at the mountain in the center of the island.

"What's going on, Nosewise?"

"I smell them—and the worm sprites too."

"You mean those monsters they've got?"

"Yes, they all came through here," I said, snuffling down the trail.

"I don't understand. Why is it warm? Did they cast a spell?"

"Broke a spell, I think." The scent of magic was weaker

here than it was on the rest of the island. "The winter weather must be Nivian's magic."

"Powerful stuff," Arthur said, hobbling after me in his hunched position.

"And Oberon's worm sprites have been eating it. That's what this path is. They've eaten the enchantment out of this little tunnel. So we can feel the weather we ought to be having."

"A summer path," Arthur said, color returning to his cheeks.

"It will lead us right to them."

The summer path was strange. Walls of snow on either side of us contained frozen leaves, roots, and dead animals, preserved in the same condition as when they were buried. Frozen forests dripped cold water on us from the low-hanging branches, which had disenchanted and were melting in the summer heat.

And then we came upon a rocky valley. At the center of it was a huge hill of packed snow, with big boulders mixed in with the ice. I looked up and saw that it was easily twice as large as Oberon's castle. Enormous rocks blocked the way on either side, and the summer path led right through it.

"That's amazing," Arthur said as we approached the icy

hill. The worm sprites had bored a hole directly into the center.

"Like earthworms eating through an apple." Arthur's voice echoed as we entered the tunnel. We walked deeper into the castle of ice, and it grew darker. I focused on the sensation of warm sunlight, and my Asteria brightened, casting a glow against the chilly walls.

"They're melted smooth," Arthur said, running his hands against them. The tunnel walls weren't cut in a straight line, but in a wavy path—the kind the worm sprites made as they swam through the air.

"They've eaten a lot of magic here," I said. "I wonder if they've grown."

"I don't like being inside this place," Arthur said, not listening. "There's a lot of weight above us in snow and rocks. It's bound to settle soon and crush whatever is inside. See there—cracks!"

Arthur pointed to long, thin fissures that zigzagged across the walls like lightning bolts.

"Let's be quick!" I shouted, and picked up to a trot. Arthur jogged behind me, and our feet squished against the muddy ground.

Soon we were out again, and my Asteria paled in the light of the sun. We looked back at the enormous fortress of snow the worm sprites had drilled through, and both of us shuddered.

*   *   *

Arthur crouched down and put a hand on my neck. "See that?" he whispered.

We'd come close to the mountain at the center of the island. The sun was setting, and my eyes hurt from the white snow we'd been staring at all day. I squinted at the wide, rocky base, but I could only make out trees and rocks.

"Left of the big round boulder. Just below the stand of three tall trees." Arthur stretched his hand at my eye level. "Firelight!"

Yes, there was a light. Hidden deep in the rocky folds at the mountain's foot, shadows were casting about the boulders. The actual flames were hidden, but the shadows were shaped like men.

"It's them, isn't it?" Arthur said. He didn't sound pleased to have found them.

A vision of the snarling worm sprites flashed before my mind, along with soldiers' swords and Oberon's toothy grin. I tried to focus on Merlin and Morgana, who were among them, and *both* needed rescuing. But part of me wanted to turn back and run.

30

My Very Good Idea

"I KNOW WHAT TO DO!" I WHISPERED AFTER THE SUN WENT down. We were hidden behind a boulder a quarter mile from the flickering camp. Arthur had insisted we couldn't approach while the soldiers were all awake. With fighting men on alert and three worm sprites ready to eat my magic, we were better off waiting until they slept.

"What is it?" Arthur turned to me stiffly. We had to wait away from the summer path to stay hidden, and I couldn't cast any more fires without attracting the worms and the guards. Arthur looked miserably cold.

"I know a way we can get past the guards!"

"Yes. Wh-what's the way?" Arthur asked, teeth chattering.

"I can make us invisible!"

He gave me a wary look. "Really?"

"I can try," I answered. "Magic is strong here. The other times I've cast spells, I've been desperate or needed a lot of concentration. But on this island it just flows out of me!"

"Fire flows out of you, and not very accurately. I remember when you cast that rotting spell on the ropes in the Fae camp. That's why I only have half a shirt!" He held up his bare, frozen arms, and my ears pressed to the sides of my head.

"That was a mistake, but how else can we get past the guards? I can't use magic near them or the worms will wake and get me."

Arthur closed his eyes and nodded. Or at least his head moved—perhaps he was only shivering.

"Have you done invisibility before?" he asked.

"No," I answered. "But once I watched Merlin in the study as he disappeared a cabbage."

"He disappeared it, or he made it invisible?"

"What's the difference?"

"There's a very big difference, Nosewise," Arthur whispered. "Did the cabbage come out all right?"

"I don't know," I answered, thinking back. "I never saw it again."

Arthur shivered.

I focused all of my attention on a small rock by our feet. I'd done illusion magic already when I'd made Oberon's leaf smell like a flower. Now all I had to do was make this rock look like nothing at all.

I struggled to find the mental image that agreed with invisibility. I settled on still air, as that was an invisible thing, and I searched my feelings for the strongest Certainty I could find.

I will save my master, Merlin.

My Asteria glowed brightly and chimed. I felt the powerful magic of the island rise up through my feet and pour into the shiny stone around my neck. My whiskers twitched, and I felt tingling on my face. I closed my eyes against the sensation.

Crack! There was a sound like breaking crystal, and when I opened my eyes again, the rock was gone.

"What did you do to it?" Arthur asked.

I pawed at the empty air and felt the rock.

"It's invisible!" I whispered as loud as I dared. "I did it!"

"It's not invisible," Arthur said, scrutinizing the empty space where the stone was. He squinted his eyes and exposed his teeth. I bent down to the spot as well. I could see the depression in the grass below it, but the stone was as see-through as air.

"What are you talking about?"

"You did make it look funny," Arthur answered. "It's blurry like a smudge on a piece of glass, and differently colored. But it almost sticks out more now."

"Sticks out?" I said, incredulous. "I can't see it at all! There's something wrong with your eyes."

"Or wrong with yours," Arthur answered, not unkindly.

"You can smell things I can't. Maybe I can see things that are invisible to you."

"That's—that's not fair," I said. "I did it right. I made the stone invisible."

"To your eyes, maybe. But not to mine."

I remembered the tests Morgana had given me in the Outdoor Study. She'd told me I couldn't see things the way she could, but I hadn't believed her.

"It was my first try. I'll do it again."

"All right," Arthur said. "But be careful. It made a noise."

"It'll be quick," I said, dropping into my Mind's Nose. I focused on still air again and found my Certainty.

The magic of the island rose up through my feet. I could feel its power pulsing through me—it was intense. My eyes closed, and I felt the Asteria vibrating.

Crack! I opened my eyes again and saw that not only was the rock invisible, but a whole chunk of grass and earth beneath it was too! It was like I'd dug a hole, but I could step on it with my paw and feel the invisible ground. It looked like I was floating.

"Amazing . . . ," I whispered.

"It didn't work," Arthur said again. "It looks like the patch of ground is made of fog. Can you really not see that?"

"I'll try again!" I said, and dropped into my Mind's Nose. *Crack! Crack! Crack!*

I could feel the powerful magic working its way through my Asteria, but I didn't know how to direct it. How could I fool Arthur if I didn't know how he saw?

"It's all right, Nosewise. We'll find another way."

"But how?" I asked. Half the boulder behind Arthur was invisible to me, and deep patches of grass looked completely disappeared.

"I don't know," he said. The starlight cast a soft glow on his face, but his eyes were hard. "I could try to distract the guard. Make a diversion so you're free to find Merlin and give him the stone."

A dark shadow passed over his face.

"What was that?" I said, looking up.

"What?"

Another shadow flew above us. A long, slithering shadow that blocked out a stream of stars.

Behind me I heard a snarl.

I turned and saw a large beast hovering just above the grass. It was as long as a man is tall and thick as a tree. Its skin was slimy and white like ash, and two glowing eyes topped a snout with long whiskers.

Arthur gasped and leapt back against the boulder. The monster snapped at the air, and I said, "Run!"

We turned and saw another beast—same as the first, but gray. It swirled down from the air above our heads and blocked our way, curling its body into a sickle shape to keep us against the boulder.

"D-dragons!" Arthur shouted. Their mouths were full of sharp teeth, and gill-like openings glowed at their sides. They swam through the air like eels and snarled at us.

"Do something, Nosewise!"

I dropped into my Mind's Nose and smelled the scent of a furious fire. Heat gathered at my chest, and a blast of flame shot forward. The white dragon roared and opened its mouth. The fireball hit it in the teeth, but it didn't burn it; instead the dragon chomped and the flame disappeared. Smoke curled around its mouth and I watched it shiver.

Did I not do it right?

The gray dragon slithered near, licking its lips.

In my Mind's Nose I sensed a strong wind. The magic of the island came through me like a hurricane, and a powerful force blasted out of my Asteria, blowing snow and ice everywhere.

The gray dragon turned, and the icy wind exploded against its side. The dragon's gills flexed, and the beast turned to me, panting with hunger.

"Arthur, these aren't dragons—"

The white one lunged at us and we dove. The beast bit hard into the boulder where I'd made it invisible—pulverizing it and leaving behind disenchanted chunks of rock.

Behind us I heard soldiers stirring.

The worm sprites had grown enormous on the magic of the Lady's island. They each finished picking through the remains of my spells and turned to me at once—eyes fixed on my glowing Asteria.

"You've got to hide, Arthur!" I shouted, backing away. "You've got to run!"

I caught one terrified glimpse of him before I turned and charged down the rocky hill. I could hear the swift sprites cutting through the air behind me.

My Asteria glowed in the night and led them on. They liked the snack I'd given them; now they wanted the meal.

31

Flight

MY FEET THUMPED LOUDLY AGAINST THE SPONGY GRASS AS I pounded down the summer trail. It was easier to run on the melted path. Behind me I could hear the unnatural sounds of the worm sprites sucking snowy enchantments through their gills.

In my Mind's Nose I focused on the scent of our burning house, and the Asteria belched black smoke.

Please hide me, I thought, and charged into an evergreen forest that appeared at the bottom of the hill. I wished the trees were thicker, but they would have to do.

My Asteria spewed ash, and I barreled over fallen logs and ducked beneath low branches. My legs were burning and my mouth was parched.

My head was thick with smoke, and I felt tired and weak. A quarter mile into the forest, I saw the hollowed-out trunk of a cedar tree off the summer trail and jumped inside. I tucked myself into its dark chamber and peeked out.

I'd shrouded the trees with thick smoke, and the ashy mists passed between branches like hair through a comb.

My thoughts turned to Arthur. *Did the soldiers hear us from the camp? Will he be able to get away?*

My Asteria was beaming light into the smoky haze. I pressed my chin to my neck to cover it, and everything darkened.

I sniffed the air, trying to sense if the worm sprites were near.

There was a sucking sound.

I peeked my head out from the hollow of the tree trunk. The smoke was thinning between the trees. I could see the dark mists moving in a single direction—up.

The worm sprites were dancing above the branches. The gray one had doubled in size; the greedy white one had tripled. My magic was too powerful here—it only helped them grow. They were sucking up my ash cloud like a drink through a straw. The white one paused midflight. It spotted me.

I leapt out and found the summer trail again. Above me I heard them shriek and swoop. I glanced back and saw them chase me. They weaved between the trees, bending thick branches and trailing needles in their wake.

They were gaining on me; I could run just barely as fast as they flew. In desperation, I spun around and blasted a ball of fire at them. It exploded against a stand of pine trees and set them ablaze. The worms swung around and chomped the burning trees. They ate them ravenously, crunching the thick trunks with their jaws. Flaming timber fell all around, and the worm sprites lapped it up.

I'd distracted them. They were hungry for magic, and I could feed it to them to slow them down. But I knew I couldn't bait them forever.

As I was reaching the forest's edge, I could hear them coming for me again. Their bodies crashed against the trees as they struggled to make their way through. The summer trail left the forest and approached a rocky expanse—giant boulders and an enormous hill of ice and stone rising into the air. A dark tunnel was bored through the center of it.

I was back at the ice fortress the worm sprites had drilled. How long had I been running?

I dropped into my Mind's Nose and sensed warm sunlight. I focused on my Certainty.

I want to live.

My Asteria hummed, and an orb of bright light flashed from my chest. It was blinding and cast my shadow all the way down the hill. I watched the glowing ball float up and up above my head and heard trees crack in the forest behind me.

Then the worms appeared.

I raced down the summer path so fast I felt the shocks in my spine. My paws were packed with painful wedges of snow, but I turned back and saw the worms swimming up through the air toward the orb of light. My magic had turned them from monsters to giants; they were nearly thirty feet long and growing bigger.

I reached the mouth of the tunnel and pawed at my collar. It was the Asteria they wanted, and they'd tear me apart trying to get it. My stupid paws couldn't knock it off, so I looked for something to catch it on. I shot an orb of light ahead of me and ran through the frozen tunnel, trying to find a jagged piece of ice, but everything was melted smooth.

There were grinding, scraping sounds behind me. I turned and saw that the worm sprites were pressed together and struggling between the tight walls of the cave. They'd grown so much bigger since they'd carved the tunnel that morning. I'd fed them so much magic. They were barely getting through.

Their bodies glowed with magical auras, which lit up the cracked tunnel walls. I remembered Arthur's worries about the weight from snow and rocks above our heads. It gave me an idea.

I stopped running and turned to them. The worm sprites screeched and roared toward me. I dropped into my Mind's Nose and conjured the most vivid scent I could imagine: the pure essence of magic, the kind I smelled straight from Merlin's Asteria.

I want to live!

Avalon's magic came up through my feet. My spine charged and my mind went white. Swift streams of particles shot out of me in a twirling arc. The energy braided and swayed, filling the ice cave with light. The worm sprites widened their mouths, drinking in the wild magic. Gills flared and leaked mist as their bodies overloaded with nourishment.

I felt the whole of the island flowing through me, dousing them with everything it had. The sprites cried out, and their bodies bloated like baking bread. Their heads and necks swelled, their eyes bulged, and their tongues thickened and overflowed from their mouths.

The sound of cracking ice clogged the chamber. The walls vibrated, and fissures zigzagged across the ceilings. The worm sprites moaned and snapped at my head, but they were stopped short—they had grown too big and were stuck in the narrow tunnel just feet in front of me.

The enormous white and gray sprites squirmed against each other and writhed, but they couldn't budge. More magic surged from my Asteria, growing them further in impossible directions.

Ice chunks rained down from the ceiling above my head. The walls snapped in jagged shapes, and I let go of my connection to the island. The worm sprites' screams echoed in my ears as I turned and raced through the collapsing chamber. Behind me ice and rock crashed, and I exploded out into the moonlight.

The entire fortress of ice had settled itself into the tunnel, and drifts of snow dust cascaded down in harmless sheets.

The worm sprites were trapped beneath. But I was on the wrong side of a ridge of enormous icy rocks.

*   *   *

By the time I'd scaled the boulders, cold sunlight filtered down on my head.

Already dawn.

I ran over the icy grass, up the hills, and through the forest. I'd survived the worms' attack, but cursed myself for getting trapped and letting the night go by. Where was Arthur? Where were Merlin and Morgana?

They were gone. I came back to the boulder where I'd hidden with Arthur and smelled soldiers everywhere. There were holes in the rocks and ground where the worm sprites had bitten out my enchantments, and a scent trail led me directly to the camp at the mountain's base.

The tents were all there, but abandoned. The fires had been snuffed out and everyone had moved on. I found Arthur, Merlin, Morgana, and Oberon among the scents of soldiers marching up the mountain, toward the top.

And I followed my nose skyward.

3 2

The Shrine in the Pines

I PANTED AND HEAVED. THE AIR GREW COLDER AS I CLIMBED UP the mountain, but the scent trail grew hotter.

My back legs pounced and my front legs caught me. My back legs launched and my front legs set up the next leap. I scaled the rocks at a full-power run.

My Asteria helped. I cast tiny shock waves at the stones directly beneath my feet. I laid down my Certainty with each pounce.

I will fight for my friends.

Boom! A blast from my Asteria cracked the ice beneath my back feet and sent me forward, fast. My bones rattled with each shock, but my concentration was sharp as a tooth.

I tried the Certainty *I will save my friends*, but I couldn't make it work. I knew Oberon had one worm sprite left. And twenty soldiers to fight for him. I tried not to think about that.

I will fight made me feel Certain. I would fight for them as long as I lived.

Boom! My Asteria blasted the rocks behind me and I gasped for breath.

Boom! The snow blew away and my ears flailed wildly.

Boom! My body soared through the air, outstretched like a bounding deer. I came down on the rocky path, and ice crystals cracked beneath my feet.

Below me the entire island of Avalon spread. It was a snowy wonderland surrounded by gentle waters. Above me was the top of a mountain with soldiers armed and ready to kill. And I was going up.

The spiraling path up the side of the mountain leveled off into a flat plateau. Tall fir and pine trees rose up as guardians of the path, and a trail of two dozen footprints in the snow weaved between them. The tops of the trees reached high above my head, and I paused for a brief moment to catch the scents of wild animals on the wind. I thought about a time when tracking squirrels through the woods was my favorite pleasure. Now I tracked Fae and men with swords.

Can't think of that, I scolded myself. *Need to keep my Certainty.*

Quicker than I expected, I came on the scene. The snow-heavy trees opened up into a quiet clearing, too quiet for a small army, but there were twenty soldiers lined up in a row. Each wore full armor: leather and metal from their feet to the tops of their heads.

Every soldier's eye was fixed on a tremendous structure that rose in the center of the clearing. I thought it was a church at first, but it was really just a giant boulder, one as big as any building I'd seen.

All along the boulder's sides and top were carvings of animals and men. The entire front of the rock had been shaped into a rough staircase, which was why I'd thought it looked like a church.

At the top of the stairs stood Merlin, with a woman beside him. *No, not a woman,* I realized. *A figure made of stone.* It was some kind of altar. The female figure rose right out of the rock, and in her hands she held a gleaming sword. Her stony fingers wrapped around the blade and offered the hilt to anyone who cared to take it.

Merlin stood stock-still beside the statue, clasping his staff. Oberon had given it back to him.

"Wizard," called an iron voice from the line of soldiers. "Retrieve for me . . . my blade."

My eyes shot back down to the base of the boulder. Oberon, in his Lord Destrian disguise, stood in the center of the formation of men. Beside him were two small figures: Arthur and Morgana. Oberon's iron gauntlets gripped Arthur around the neck. I couldn't see Morgana's face, but her whole body was trembling.

Where is the worm? I thought. I glanced across the crowd and saw a soldier at the far corner. A chain led from his shaking hand to what seemed to be a fallen log on the ground. It was the wood-colored worm sprite. It rested peacefully in the snow, soaking up what it could of the island's magic.

My ears flattened and I crouched low to the ground. *How can I fight them?* A small army of men carried swords. The worm sprite ate magic. Oberon was a better sorcerer by far.

"Wizard, hear my words and . . ." Oberon's iron voice stumbled as he tried to twist his speech into a more human form. "Deliver the sword of kings. For the glory of . . . my name!"

"Destrian! Destrian!" the soldiers shouted, slamming their fists on their leather armor. "King! King!"

Their voices scared me and my tail drooped. There were so many of them. I lowered farther in the snow.

"You are no king of mine, and I will never grant you this sword. If you want it so badly, you must try for yourself!" Merlin said from the top of the stone altar. His voice quivered and he glanced at the resting worm sprite. "If you threaten me with death, I accept. I surrender my life for the good of the realm."

My ears shot up at that, and my whole stomach turned over. Would Merlin really let Oberon kill him?

I will save my master, I thought, trying to conjure a sense of Certainty. But I wasn't Certain I could.

"It is not your life . . . that you will . . . surrender," Oberon called in his twisted, iron voice. His gauntleted hand grasped Arthur tighter by the neck, and Arthur screamed. Oberon raised him up off the ground so his feet thrashed in the air.

"It is his!" Oberon drew a dagger from his belt and pressed it to Arthur's throat.

I tried to shout, but my throat was hoarse. I tried to run, but I was frozen to the ground. The men and their swords made me cower, and Oberon's echoing voice crowded my mind.

Arthur's in danger, I thought. *I will save him!*

The words were like wisps of smoke on the wind. They disappeared in the terror that gripped me. Oberon's hands held Arthur by the neck, and, weirdly, I felt them clamping down on my own. Nivian's Asteria, which had given me power, was being poisoned by my fear. Its magic closed my throat and stopped my breath.

"Don't do it, Merlin!" Arthur shouted, and his voice echoed in the chamber of my mind. "I lay down my life too!" he screamed through fear and pain. "I lay down my life!"

The sides of my vision collapsed until the scene was a narrow tunnel. I saw Merlin flinch, but he would not move.

Oberon grunted and threw Arthur to the ground. I blinked hard when I saw him hit the snow. He coughed and tried to raise himself, but Oberon put a heavy boot on his back.

"If your own life . . . means nothing to you," Oberon said in his stilted human tongue, "and this boy's neither . . . then I'll do as you once said—and take hers!"

Oberon pressed Arthur deep into the snow and switched his knife into the other hand. He turned as quick as a snake and snatched up Morgana, who'd been trembling at his side.

"No! Father, stop!" she screamed as he lifted her high in the air and pressed the blade against her chest. "No!"

Merlin's mouth went wide. "Don't hurt her!" he shouted. "All right! I'll break the spell."

Morgana sobbed and Merlin raised his staff above the statue—the Asteria within glowing bright.

"I'll plunge my knife into her chest!" Oberon shouted, the music slipping back into his voice. "I am not a soul to test!"

Merlin brought his staff down onto the sword in the statue's hands. Lightning and fire erupted where the Asteria met the golden hilt. Bright flames lit Merlin's face as it twisted in pain. He shook and cried out. The whole of the Sword in the Stone glowed hot—the air around it pulsed with power. My jaws clenched and ground my teeth.

Merlin was dying in front of me. Morgana had a knife to her chest. Arthur was being crushed into freezing snow.

I tried to wake myself from the living nightmare, but fear kept me bound in place. My Certainties were poisoned ones:

My friends will die.

I've failed them all.

I'll never see Merlin again.

They pressed me down. My body grew cold. My mind went blank.

*   *   *

Nosewise, sounded a voice from far off in the distance, across the dark and snowy plain.

Nosewise, spoke the voice again, simple and familiar. There was a lilt of music in the words, and when she called my name, I heard something more.

Nosewise, said Nivian, the Lady of the Lake. I could hear her clearly now. *Who are they?* she said, and the question confused me.

Who? I asked with my last strength.

Those before you, Nivian answered, her voice guiding me to the only corner of my mind not in shadow. *Merlin, Arthur, and Morgana*, she said. *Who are they?*

My master, I thought. *A boy I met along the way. A friend who betrayed me.*

No. Nivian's voice beckoned me on. *Who are they in your heart?*

And in that last small corner—in a tiny speck of light the Lady showed me still remained—I found an answer.

They are my family, I thought. *And I love them, every one.*

It was a very Certain thought.

33

My Certainty

"Merlin, stop!" I shouted, my voice unleashed. The darkness in my mind cleared and the stone's power returned to me.

Merlin's gaunt face turned and spotted me across the field. I saw his eyebrows jump in surprise, and his staff lifted from the sword. The hilt, which had been glowing bright and sparking fire, died down to embers. The sword stayed in the stone, its enchantment unbroken.

Merlin mouthed something, maybe my name, and collapsed on the altar. "Merlin!" I shouted, and sprang forward.

Oberon turned to face me, dropping Morgana to the ground. She yelped and crawled away. He was wearing Lord Destrian's face and scowled as he grabbed the war hammer off his back. Soldiers unsheathed their swords and aimed crossbows in my direction.

I had no plan. I simply ran forward. I didn't know if I

could succeed. I didn't know if I would live. But I was Certain of my love, and that was enough to make me run.

A shrieking cry sounded, and I saw the wood-colored worm sprite struggling against its chain. The soldier held it back from the magic that fizzled around the sword.

I stopped and spread my legs wide in the snow. I felt the Lady's presence in the cold grass and welcomed her.

That pure form of magic welled in my Asteria again. It felt like an old friend.

I sent a blast of wild magic directly at Oberon and his swinging war hammer. It broke against his armor plate and spun out in a dozen directions, like water splashed against a stone.

Someone shouted to my right—the soldier had lost control of the chain. The wood-colored worm sprite screeched through the crowd, consuming the shiny white gobs of magic. Its jaws clamped down and its tail whipped, knocking armored men everywhere. Swords and crossbows left their hands and stuck in the snowy ground. The monster charged by Oberon, knocking out his legs.

Soldiers screamed and steel flashed through the sky. I saw glimpses of Arthur and Morgana in the chaos, and my hairs stood on end. I charged into the fray, dodging fists and boots that struck out at me.

I found Arthur in a mound of snow. "Arthur!" I shouted.

"Get up!" I licked his face and his eyes focused on mine. I nudged my snout beneath his arm and he pushed himself up by my shoulder. Behind us I heard a grunt, and I turned to see a soldier charging with a sword.

I grounded myself and barked, my Certainty never out of my mind.

My blast of shock knocked the man off his feet and into the soft snow. The worm sprite turned to me and snarled. I focused deeply and sent another shot of wild magic into a group of five soldiers picking up their weapons. The airy substance broke against their bodies and flurried about like snowflakes. The worm sprite swerved and took off in their direction. Some soldiers dropped their weapons and ran. The others were knocked into the air.

"Nosewise, you're alive," Arthur said, clutching my face. "How did you—"

"We've got to help Merlin!" I shouted, glancing at the chaotic scene. Merlin was slumped against the statue at the top of the altar. The fighting men were in chaos, but where was Oberon? I'd lost sight of Morgana too.

Arthur gasped and his face went pale.

"Nosewise, behind!" he said, pointing over my shoulder. "Destrian!"

Oberon was there, his armor brighter than the snow, his war hammer propped against his shoulder casually, like nothing was amiss. He walked toward me slowly as his men screamed and ran behind him.

"Arthur, go to Merlin!" I said. "I'll deal with him!"

"But, Nosewise—"

"Go, I said!"

Arthur nodded and scrambled up the carved stairs of the altar. I turned back to see Oberon's hammer high above his head. With a shout, he brought it down.

I leapt to the side and heard the heavy metal crash into the stone. I turned back and saw that the bottom stair of the altar was shattered. Oberon lifted the heavy weapon like it weighed nothing at all and turned to me.

"My quarrel is not with dogs, but men," Oberon said to me, the Fae music fully filling his voice, though he was still wearing his human face. "Why do you show yourself again?"

He brought the hammer down on the patch of ice and snow I stood on. Again I dodged it, just in time to see the damage it would have done me.

"You were going to kill my master!" I shouted, scampering away. A group of three soldiers had found their weapons and slashed at me when I ran near them. The worm sprite swooped by, chasing rogue bits of magic.

"Are you troubled by that still?" Oberon shouted, swinging his war hammer at my head. "Are you one more I have to kill?"

I ducked the heavy hammerhead and felt the iron clip my ears with a sting. I darted away but was blocked by another group of men. They charged me. "Devil!" one screamed, hurling his sword at my face. It pierced the frozen ground, and slush sprayed me.

I barked and sent a blast of shock that knocked them off their feet. The worm sprite hissed and spun, but a mote of wild magic floated past, and it chased that instead. Oberon bore down on me.

"If you hate men, why do you pretend to be one?" I sputtered at him desperately. There were more soldiers behind me—frightened men, I could tell. They feared the worm sprite and me. But they'd strike me if I came too close. Oberon advanced; his bravery egged them on.

I glanced around. There was a circle of men now, at least a dozen, closing in on all sides.

"Devil!" they shouted.

"Evil spirit!"

"Purge the demon!"

"Is this all you can do?" I goaded Oberon. "Where's your magic?"

The worm was almost finished with its meal. It would come for my Asteria next. But if I could trick Oberon into casting a spell, it would be drawn to him instead.

"I practice no . . . devilry," Oberon said, trying to compress his voice into human speech. "My armor, you see, gleams true and bright!" he shouted, raising his hammer high. The sound of music flooded back. "For I am a lord of the light!"

His hammer came down hard and fast, and I braced myself, having nowhere left to run. *Bing!* A sound like a gong struck hard above my head. I peered up and saw Oberon's hammer stopped in midair and vibrating like a bell. Then a snowy blast of wind blew him into the broken bottom stair of the altar.

"Nosewise, get down!" shouted a frightened voice. From out of the snow Morgana appeared, her open hand outstretched. I saw that her Asteria had been reset into a bracelet, which weaved between her fingers and held the magic stone in the center of her palm. The stone glowed with heat.

Above me blasts of fire shot out at the soldiers, and they screamed, retreating from the frightening blaze. I peeked up through my furry eyebrows and was shocked at what Morgana was doing. I'd never seen her cast a spell so powerful.

The armed men backed off, and Morgana ran to me, pulling me up from the snow.

"How did you do that?" I asked, amazed.

"Oh, Nosewise!" she cried, throwing her arms around my neck. "I've found my Certainty." Tears streamed down her cheeks. I saw her eyes and knew that her Certainty was the same as mine.

Behind us there was a terrible screech. The wood-colored worm sprite had eaten the last of my magic. It was overfed and enormous now, nearly thirty feet long and as thick as a barrel. I was afraid to feed it any more. There was no tunnel to trap it in here. The more I grew it, the harder it would be to fight.

It looked around lazily. On top of the altar, Arthur was trying to revive Merlin and get him to his feet. Merlin's staff and Asteria lay on the stone, cold and untouched. All around us fighting men were in various states of confusion, injury, and fear. They didn't have any magic. Oberon groaned in his polished armor, pushing himself up against the stony stairs.

Then the beast settled on the two of us: me with an Asteria around my neck that had produced delicious magic, and Morgana with a stone that still glowed from the fire. I watched its eyes make a decision for Morgana. It slithered into the air and swooped down at us.

"Morgana," I said. "Throw your Asteria away!"

She turned to me, still blinking tears from her eyes. "But I can't— My magic! I've just regained the power—"

"Trust me, Morgana. Throw it away!"

The worm sprite was flying for us fast. Morgana hesitated, sucking air through her teeth, and I barked at her.

"All right!" she shouted, taking hold of the stone with her free hand and ripping it off the setting. Then she reared back and hurled the Asteria into the snow.

The worm sprite's head turned, following the stone. We ducked beneath the worm and watched it rise again above us. Just then I saw Oberon stand and grip his hammer, Lord Destrian's golden wings stretching from his helmet.

I had an idea. I focused my Certainty and sent a ball of fire to the distant end of the altar. The worm sprite followed the burning spell, but I knew it wouldn't take long to eat something so weak.

I ran to Morgana's Asteria and snatched it up in my jaws. Oberon walked to me, swinging his hammer.

I let Morgana's Asteria, which had once been mine, sit between my teeth. I felt its power flow through me, and I thanked it for all it had done. The island's power rushed into it, and it glowed in my mouth like a miniature sun.

"Nosewise, what are you doing?" Morgana shouted. "The sprite!"

Oberon lowered his hammer and said in the stilted voice of a man, "Your magic can't help you now . . . demon."

"No," I answered through the stone between my teeth, "I'm just a dog." I heard a screech; the sprite was coming for me.

"And magic is for those with the wisdom to wield it!" I murmured, and flung the hot Asteria at Oberon. The bright white stone sailed through the air and thumped against his chest. Reflexively he cupped his hands—and caught it.

Crash! The worm sprite slammed into Oberon's heavy armor, plowing him into the ground and snapping viciously at his chest, face, and hands.

"Let's go to Merlin!" I shouted at Morgana. She stared at the enormous beast as it floated above her supposed father, its tail thirty feet in the air and its jaws coming down again and again against the heavy armor. I ran to her and nosed her neck. She shook her head and followed me to the altar. We passed by Destrian's men, dazed and frightened by the magic they'd seen.

The two of us clambered up the steep stairs to the top, where Arthur bent over Merlin.

"Merlin!" I cried. He was huddled against the statue and breathing heavily. "Are you all right?"

"Master, I'm sorry!" Morgana shouted, falling to his side. "Merlin, can you hear me?"

Arthur turned to us; his face was cut and he looked half-frozen. "He's alive," he said. "But weak. He told me to leave and run, but I wouldn't."

"None of us will leave you, Merlin," I said, putting a paw to his chest and licking his face.

"None of us," Morgana echoed, grabbing hold of his hand. "We'll keep you safe."

Arthur gave Morgana an angry look, but I whined and he turned to me instead. "How are we going to do that?"

I looked around. The statue of the woman holding the sword stood tall at our left. From this close I could see how delicate and lifelike her features were. In fact, the statue was a likeness of Nivian exactly, but carved from stone. The sword still rested in her hand, glowing dimly with whatever enchantment kept it locked there.

I stood and peered over the back of the altar. We were surrounded by tall, heavy trees on all sides. By the shouts, snarls, and screams down below, I could tell that Oberon and his soldiers were still in chaos. We could run down the rear of the altar, into the trees, down the mountain—all the way to the shore, where Nivian's boat waited to rescue us.

But Merlin can't run. Arthur and Morgana crouched over him, whispering encouragements and begging him to stand.

The screeches stopped; nearly all sound ceased at the base of the altar. Maybe the worm sprite had finished them off, or scared them away. I ran to the top of the stairs and looked down.

Oberon was on the ground, but he had gained hold of the worm sprite's chain. The beast was forty feet long. I guessed it had eaten Morgana's Asteria. Oberon calmed the sprite, stroking it with his long-nailed hand.

He was unmasked. The sprite had torn off his helmet and his armor down to the waist. The glamour over his face was gone, and his glowing eyes and skin reflected off the snow. His oaky antlers were on full display, but one was snapped, hanging by a thread and bleeding.

His soldiers stood around him, awed. One broke the silence.

"By the stars!" he exclaimed.

"He's a monster!" cried another.

"A Fae!"

Some cowered; some gawked at the Fae. I glanced back at Merlin—he still couldn't stand.

The scene below grew loud, chaotic. *Maybe they'll abandon him,* I hoped. *Maybe they'll just go away.*

Oberon coldly considered his panicking soldiers. He tenderly reset his broken antler and held it in place. Then he groaned and rose to his feet. His height and appearance frightened the men back into silence. He considered them and calmly stroked the forty-foot beast that swayed by his side.

"I am a Fae and lord of the wood. I took my guise for man's own good." He spoke in his natural voice, musical and lyrical. The men around him gaped. "I have laid claim to this foolish realm"—he closed his fists, and it seemed like he had his hand around every soldier's heart—"and bless it with my steady hand upon the helm."

I looked at the faces of the fighting men. Oberon's words were working their power on them. Their fear was repressed, and their eyes grew eager.

"I've raised you up; I can bring you down," he said, locking eyes with each man. His naked chest rippled with power. "I'll remember you when I have my crown. Death will come to those who betray me, and riches to those who know to obey me."

Oberon was silent. The worm sprite screeched. He raised his glance to me, and slowly each and every soldier turned. They bent down to pick swords out of the snow. They crouched low and fixed me with angry stares.

Oberon had his army again.

I ran back to my friends at the base of the statue.

34

The Sword in the Stone

"MERLIN, THEY'RE COMING FOR US! YOU'VE GOT TO TELL US what to do!"

I pushed between Arthur and Morgana and stuck my nose right in Merlin's face. He blinked at me and crinkled his eyebrows.

"Who is?" Merlin asked. His eyes looked far away. "Tell them I'm taking a bath. Come by later."

My jaw dropped, and I looked between Arthur and Morgana. Merlin couldn't help us.

"Is it the soldiers or Oberon?" Arthur asked.

"Or the worm sprite?" Morgana said, her voice ragged and panicked.

"All of them," I answered, glancing over my shoulder. "They're all coming. If we want to survive it—we've got to fight."

"Fight with what?" Arthur asked, showing his empty hands.

"I don't have my Asteria," Morgana said. She touched her palm where it had been.

"I've got mine," I answered. "And you can take Merlin's!" I pointed my nose at Merlin's staff on the ground.

"I can't use his Asteria," Morgana said, looking at the knotty staff. Merlin had always kept it on a high hook out of Morgana's reach.

I bent down and picked up the gnarly thing between my teeth. "You have to," I said through the wood, and dropped it in her lap.

Morgana held her hands above the staff and the Asteria glowed. She grasped the handle and it chimed like a bell.

"There you are," Merlin mumbled faintly. "Good girl."

Morgana shot him a desperate look.

"But what about the worm thing?" Arthur shouted. "Won't it eat the magic?"

"Yes," I said, not having thought it through. "These aren't enough. We need more." I glanced at Arthur and caught his eyes. "You need to pull the sword."

"Do *what?*" Arthur answered.

"Pull the Sword in the Stone."

"I can't do that," Arthur said, turning to Morgana for explanation.

"You can," I said, stepping on Arthur's knee. "You're the worthy soul. I know it. The Lady in the Lake practically told me so. Pull the sword and use it to fight."

Behind us we heard a screech. The worm sprite was coming.

"Distract it with spells!" I said to Morgana. She leapt up and leveled Merlin's staff with a steady hand. "And, Arthur, pull the sword!"

Morgana and I ran to the top edge of the altar. The worm sprite was slithering through the air above the steps. Oberon and the soldiers advanced steadily behind it.

I dropped into my Mind's Nose and focused on my Certainty. The scent of fire burned within me.

I barked ferociously and a fireball sprung from my Asteria. It blasted down toward Oberon and his men. The worm sprite swiftly switched its course and swallowed the fire whole, knocking a half-dozen soldiers to the ground.

"Keep them back!" I shouted. Morgana nodded and closed her eyes.

Blast! Great gusts of wind shot out of Merlin's staff. My tail wagged in appreciation; Morgana was alight with power. She squinted and focused her flurries at individual soldiers, knocking some down before the worm sprite could catch her magic.

Oberon cried out and pressed his hands together. A bright light flashed from between his palms, and he opened his hands to us, sending a shock that toppled us to the ground.

I popped up and peeked over the edge of the stairs. The worm sprite had turned on Oberon again and was snapping at his palms. He slapped the creature, and the soldiers cautiously made their way forward.

Morgana was at my side again, sending wind to blow the soldiers back. Some fell to their knees and others tumbled down the steps. The worm sprite whipped away from Oberon and faced us.

The party was halfway up the altar.

"What are you doing?" I yelled at Arthur. He was standing in front of the statue, looking at Nivian's stone face. "Take the sword!" I shouted.

"All right!" Arthur answered over his shoulder. He rubbed his hands together and put his foot on the carving of Nivian's knee. He gripped the hilt of the sword with both hands. The dim light that emitted from the golden handle glowed brighter for a moment. I held my breath.

He pulled and kicked against the stone.

"Ahh!" Arthur grunted, his hands coming away from the hilt. The sword stayed in Nivian's rocky grip.

"I can't!" he shouted.

"Try again!" I called, but I had to turn to fire off a volley of spells at the soldiers. Morgana had been holding our ground, shooting fire, wind, and shock to knock the soldiers away and keep the worm sprite chasing. But they'd advanced just the same. The worm sprite was even larger now, forty-five feet and as thick as a horse. Instead of chasing our spells with its jaws, it was big enough now to just float in front of the soldiers lengthwise and absorb our magic with its shivering body.

Oberon's men marched behind their barricade. The sprite floated closer, and the rest came up behind.

I turned and saw Arthur struggling desperately with the sword. His back was arched and his eyes were bulging. I could smell the fear in his sweat.

I glanced up at the stone face of the statue. It perfectly resembled the Lady of the Lake. Her eyes were made of polished rock, yet they seemed to look at me. Her carved mouth curved. *Did she smile?*

Something told me I should help Arthur pull the sword. He couldn't do it alone. Something urged me on. *Nosewise, try!*

I ran across the altar and leapt on the stone Lady's feet. Arthur grunted and pulled mightily against the hilt, and I found a place on the golden handle where my mouth could get a grip. I bit down hard, closed my eyes, and heaved.

The ground hit me unexpectedly and knocked the wind out of me. I found myself coughing, upside down in the dirt. I blinked and saw Arthur standing above me. The gold and silver sword, Excalibur, was lying by my side on the ground. Arthur gaped at it.

Excalibur glowed with ethereal light and chimed. *Like a very big Asteria*, I thought to myself, still dazed from the fall.

"The sword," I said with the little breath I had. "Pick it up."

"But—but I . . . ," Arthur stammered. "I—I didn't—"

"Pick it up!" I gasped, and saw the worm sprite rise above the top step of the altar. It was like a writhing, floating oak tree. Morgana screamed and ran backward toward Merlin, shooting spells the entire way. She hadn't noticed the sword.

Arthur's eyes went wide when he saw the sprite screeching and howling at the magic. Without looking down, he bent and picked Excalibur up from the ground. The sword rang like a bell and glowed bright in his hands.

Everything I saw was upside down. The soldiers stopped short at the top of the steps. Even Oberon hesitated and held his hands to his eyes. Excalibur's light grew blinding.

The worm sprite shrieked and spun in the air. Our spells and Asterias were of no interest anymore. Its mouth went wide and its gills opened, absorbing Excalibur's light. In its eyes I saw double reflections of the magical sword.

Swift as a snake, the worm sprite screeched toward Arthur.

"Strike it!" I yelled. Arthur shouted something I couldn't hear over the noise.

I rolled out of the beast's way and tumbled over just in time to see Arthur hold Excalibur up to the seam of the worm sprite's biting jaws.

And, like lightning cleaving a mighty oak tree, Excalibur split the monster in two halves, which spread and thundered by Arthur on either side. They curled and crashed down on the stone with a thud and were silent.

Slowly I stood up on all four legs, my Asteria dangling from my neck. Morgana raised Merlin's staff to her chest. Arthur breathed heavily and pointed Excalibur straight ahead.

The three of us stood before Oberon and the group of awestruck soldiers and prepared ourselves for battle.

3 5

The Sword in the Hand

EXCALIBUR SHOT A BEAM OF BRIGHT LIGHT FROM ITS BLADE, AND all the soldiers shielded their eyes.

"He's got the sword!" one of them exclaimed.

Oberon squinted and peered at Arthur.

"He took it himself!" another soldier said.

Oberon looked cautious. He kept his antlered head ducked near his chest and breathed heavily.

"Stay away!" I barked a soft spell of shock that knocked them back but didn't hurt them. The sprite was gone, and that was good for us, but now Oberon could use his magic without being bothered. I didn't know if a duel would go well for us.

Oberon took his eyes off the sword and shook his head. "Attack," he said, looking back at his soldiers. "Go on— take the sword from him." He spoke with force, but he made no move for us.

I remembered Nivian calling it the sword of power. I

didn't know what power it had, but I could tell that Oberon was afraid of it.

He reached out his hands to Arthur and cried, "Go!"

Arthur breathed heavily and looked to me; he had no idea what to do.

"It's powerful," I whispered. "Show them!"

Arthur nodded but held the sword stiffly. *Show them the power*, I thought, and the sword began to swing in Arthur's hands. *Yes, like that!*

"It's magic!" Morgana said, with a mix of fear and glee.

"Morgana, daughter . . ." Oberon turned to her. His face was twisted and pained; the sword was having some effect on him. "I am your lord. Fight the boy and take the sword."

"You lied to me," Morgana said. "You made me hurt Nosewise and Merlin!"

Oberon blinked. "Fight them!" he commanded his soldiers. "Quickly."

Two soldiers ran out, thrusting their swords at Arthur. Morgana and I readied spells to force them back, but before we could, Excalibur swung in Arthur's hand and knocked their weapons to the ground. Arthur closed his eyes and flinched, but still the sword moved expertly.

"The boy pulled the sword!" shouted a man in the pack. "That makes him king."

The other soldiers traded looks and nodded. They were awed by the blade's light. One by one, soldiers dropped to their knees. They laid their weapons on the ground and shielded their eyes.

For generations, humans had bowed to whoever held Excalibur. That was why Oberon wanted it so badly.

Oberon looked at them, and I'd never seen him so unsure. He pressed his hands together and closed his eyes like he was readying a spell. Then he grunted and thrust his fists—but nothing happened.

Behind me I heard soft laughter.

Merlin leaned against the unsworded statue and chuckled.

"Feeling Uncertain?" he said quietly.

Oberon raged and smashed his palms together. He charged at Arthur full tilt. He was seven feet tall, not including the antlers, and broad-shouldered. Arthur yelped and held up the sword.

Oberon pounced and grabbed the blade with his bare hands.

Excalibur sparked and flamed. Oberon screamed and staggered back. His hands were alight with fire. He dropped to his knee and pressed his hands against the stone.

"No touching!" Merlin chuckled, still in a daze.

Arthur held the blade at arm's length, frightened of it.

"Just go away," I said, and Oberon looked up at me. "My boy holds Excalibur." Arthur shook the magic sword. "My girl is a great wizard." I glanced at Morgana and she lowered her staff.

Oberon stared at me, seething. His eyes burned with unending hate.

"And I won't let you hurt my friends."

"You are nothing; you are no one," Oberon said, rising again to his full height. "Mine is the head the crown will go on." He sneered and grabbed a soldier's battle-ax off the ground. "Swords and magic cannot kill me. My desire is what *will be*. I will always be your dread, for I will hunt you till you're dead!"

Oberon hissed and bared his terrible teeth. Morgana sent a spell of shock that knocked him back. He rose again and charged. I cast flames, and he turned and pressed his face into his shoulder. Then he locked eyes with me. It wasn't working. We weren't strong enough.

Crack!

Oberon stopped short. His rage melted into fear. The soldiers behind him went wide-eyed.

Behind me, Nivian's statue was breaking apart.

Fractures spread from the stone's hands to its elbows. Cracks broke above the eyes, and the smooth, polished lips flaked off. From every break flowed a stream of sweet-smelling water. The moisture darkened the rock and ran down the surface in torrents.

Arthur gasped and stepped away. Merlin slipped.

Foamy bubbles churned at the statue's feet, and the face plate dropped off. Through the rushing waters I spotted flesh.

"Nivian," Merlin gasped.

Broken chunks of polished rock swept by our feet in the flooding current, and I looked up to see the Lady standing there.

She stepped out of what was left of the stone and strode toward Oberon.

"Little brother!" she cried, her voice echoing against the trees. "Do you come to desecrate my home?"

Oberon opened his burned hand and dropped the ax against the rock. "Nivian, no . . . I—"

"You come to steal what's mine?" she raged, light streaming from her eyes and cold water from her hands. Gushing rivers flowed from her palms, washing swords and rocks over the sides of the altar.

"A goddess!" one soldier cried.

"A Fae!" called another. "I'm not dying for this!"

Every fighting man who hadn't already been swept by the current charged down the steps, slipping and falling. They shouted and ran into the woods.

"Sister!" Oberon called. "We work toward joint ends!"

"You bring twisted creations here to eat my magic!" the Lady screamed. "Force my pupil to break my enchantment. And threaten children, Oberon! How have you fallen so low?"

"I do not threaten." He dropped to his knees and held his hands to us. "These are my friends."

"Come here," Merlin called to us, the cold water reviving his senses. Morgana, Arthur, and I struggled in the violent stream. The torrent flowed toward the edge of the altar and threatened to wash us over the stairs. The Lady was caught in a rage and ignored us. We trudged through the waves. Morgana made it to Merlin first and then held out a hand to Arthur; he grabbed her wrist and pulled himself to the ruined base of the statue. I jumped over the swelling waters and landed in Merlin's arms.

"My enchantment is broken, but not by you!" Nivian boomed over the current. "By the worthy soul."

"Sister, please," Oberon pleaded. "I did what I thought was best!"

"Your heart was fueled by fire," Nivian replied. "And the only cure I know is ice."

"No!" Oberon shouted, and turned to run.

But the water beneath his feet froze into a solid block. He tried to pull away from the magical bonds, but ice crept up his legs, into his hips and belly, and above his chest. It finally froze his face into a mask of fear.

The Lady clasped her hands, and the water stopped.

36

The Lady from the Stone

"UM . . . ARTHUR, MORGANA," I SAID, NERVOUSLY WAGGING MY tail. "This is the Lady of the Lake."

Nivian turned, her face cold and strong. Behind her, Oberon was frozen in ice. All around us the chilly water drained from the altar's top.

"Hello," Arthur said meekly.

Morgana couldn't even manage a word. She stared at the Lady in shock.

"Nivian," Merlin murmured, attempting to get up but falling on his backside again. "So good to see you." He looked between Arthur, Morgana, and me. "I think you're scaring the children," he whispered.

Nivian's body relaxed from her fighting pose. Her face seemed to warm, and she tilted her head at Arthur. "Hello, Arthur. When we met, you were not awake."

"Can't believe I missed it," Arthur answered, still in shock.

"And you," Nivian said, turning to Morgana. "I've heard

much about you." Her voice was kind, but Morgana looked crestfallen. Her eyes lowered and she murmured something beneath her breath. "What was that?" the Lady asked.

"Nothing good," Morgana said, peering up at her. "You've heard nothing good, I'm sure."

"Much good," the Lady answered. "Merlin spoke of you as a promising student. I've seen evidence of this myself."

Morgana blushed.

"Nivian, look!" Merlin said, trying to get up and falling again.

"Please just sit!" I said, scurrying to him.

He brushed me off. "Look!" he said again. "Arthur pulled Excalibur! He's the one we've been looking for!"

"He did?" Nivian asked. She turned to Arthur and he went pale. "No need to fear. May I see the sword?"

"Y-yes, ma'am," Arthur stammered, and stumbled forward, holding out Excalibur.

"Nosewise is the one who found him," Merlin said. "Sensed greatness in the boy!"

"Nosewise is a clever dog," she said, gazing down at me. "But you must give yourself credit, my student," she said to Merlin. "*You* found the one who pulled the sword from the stone."

"What?" Merlin asked. "Well, we did meet in Oberon's castle. But Nosewise brought him here."

"It's more like Arthur brought *me* here," I said, trying to ignore Oberon's frozen form behind us.

"Thank you, Arthur," said the Lady in her musical voice. "You have escorted the sword bringer to my island safely. I hope that you will carry Excalibur for Nosewise in good stead. I never thought my worthy soul might have paws instead of hands."

"I—uh, yes, ma'am." Arthur bowed his head, bewildered by the beautiful and frightening Lady of the Lake.

"Nosewise?" Morgana gasped, and she put a hand over her mouth.

"But Arthur took the sword from the stone!" said Merlin.

"What do you mean?" I asked, and pushed the Lady's forearm with my snout. "I saw him do it myself!"

"No, little Nosewise. You took the hilt and pulled it free."

"He did?" Merlin blurted out.

"No, I didn't. I only helped."

"The enchantment broke for you."

"I knew it!" Arthur said, snapping his fingers. "It wouldn't budge for me. But then Nosewise came, and it slipped right out." He turned to Merlin. "I couldn't say it without sounding stupid."

"That's what I saw too," Morgana said. "But I was afraid to say."

"Remember the prophecy," the Lady said, gently running her fingers across the base of my ears.

I panted and tried to remember. "You said a 'worthy soul' would pull the sword," I answered. "Arthur is worthy."

Merlin rubbed his chin with one hand and his brow with the other. Slowly, a smile worked its way across his face. "Only one *who loves man and would do him no harm* might take it," Merlin chanted. He laughed. "Who loves man more than a dog?"

The Lady of the Lake smiled and scratched my neck. "On the lake, I told you that the worthy soul might be before me. But you had to try the sword to make sure."

Arthur, Merlin, Morgana, and Nivian all gathered around me and petted my head. They called me good dog and kissed me and scratched my ears. I hardly knew what to say.

"Arthur will keep Excalibur safe," I finally said. "He risked his life for me and Merlin. We owe him everything." Merlin nodded at that. Morgana looked ashamed.

"Will you carry the sword for Nosewise, Arthur?" the Lady asked, offering Excalibur to him.

"I—I will, my lady," Arthur said, gripping the sword in his hand.

Morgana burst into tears. "I'm sorry!" she shouted. "This is my fault!"

"No, Morgana!" Merlin consoled her.

"He tricked you," I said, and nudged her hand. "I know what it's like to love someone so much you'd do anything."

Morgana peered at me and patted my head. Merlin held out his hand to her and she took it. They smiled at each other with glimmering eyes.

Arthur seemed to feel out of place. He kept glancing over at Oberon's frozen form. "Um, Lady of the Lake . . . ma'am . . ."

"You may call me Nivian," she corrected him.

"Right, Nivian," Arthur said, obviously uncomfortable. "What is . . . uh . . . what's happening with him?" He gestured in the direction of the statue that had a moment before been threatening to kill us.

"He's alive," Nivian said, as though this were reassuring.

"Really," Arthur answered, gripping the sword tighter and stepping away.

"I've bound him," the Lady said, considering Oberon with pity. "My brother was arrogant to think he could attack my island. His worm sprites kept my power in check, and much of my magic was tied up in holding the sword. But you killed both those birds with one stone," she said, turning to Arthur and me.

"Uh . . . glad we could do that for you?" Arthur answered awkwardly.

Morgana considered Oberon: large and intimidating, yet frozen in ice.

"He told me he was my true family and that Merlin held me back." She turned and faced us, tearful. "Why did I believe him?"

"We don't always know who we are in this world," Nivian said, her voice like sweet music. "Where we come from, what made us." She considered our gathering on the stones of the altar. "Wizards, dogs, orphans, and spirits. We find what we can in each other."

Arthur smiled at me and rested the tip of the sword on the ground. "I think I've found friends here," he said.

Merlin nodded. "Companions," he added.

"And family," I said, pressing my cheek against Morgana's hip. "That's what you'll always be to me."

37

At Home in the Hills

AFTER MERLIN WAS FEELING SOLID ON HIS FEET AGAIN, THE LADY of the Lake told us to go down the back of the mountain. She had to attend to Oberon, but she said that if we stayed on a trail she showed us, we would find a safe place to rest.

The path through the trees was not steep and led us gently down from the peak.

"I feel like I don't know where we are," Arthur said, shifting the sword from hand to hand and resting it in different positions on his shoulders. "I didn't see a trail like this when we were below."

"Yes, it looked like harder going," I said.

"Merlin, where are we headed?" Morgana asked.

"Uh . . . hmm." Merlin scratched his head. "I do seem to remember there being a secret path, maybe glamoured."

"You mean hidden?" Arthur asked.

"It's not as simple as hiding something," Morgana answered him.

Arthur still seemed wary of her. He'd seen her do some awful things. But Merlin and I had forgiven Morgana, and Arthur was outnumbered two to one.

"A glamoured path can obscure something from sight, and it can't be stumbled onto blindly," she explained with confidence. "It's like a door that can only be opened with the aid of magic."

"Very good, Morgana!" Merlin praised her. He tipped his head, and she smiled.

"Is it like the fireplace in Oberon's castle?" I asked, hoping Merlin would notice that I knew about magic too.

"Indeed it is, Nosewise," Merlin said. "Your Asteria gave you access to the secret passage. Someday I will show you how to make one yourself!"

My tail wagged at that. From now on I'd be treated as a real apprentice.

Arthur sighed audibly. "Is magic all anyone's going to talk about? Because I am *not* a wizard."

"Magic has helped you a lot," I reminded Arthur.

"Yeah, but it's nearly killed me more," Arthur answered. "I'm tired of it."

Merlin laughed and stepped lightly, hardly using his staff for support. Something about the island seemed to rejuvenate him. "You know, Arthur, that sword is quite a magical object. You might pick up a thing or two just from wielding it."

"So this really is the only topic?" Arthur said wearily.

"You might be grateful," Morgana added. "You're the owner of an amazing artifact."

"He's not really the owner," I said. It felt strange staking a claim on the sword, but the Lady had said it was mine. "But Arthur is my carrier, and he can use it too, if he wants."

"I'd be happy just finding a comfortable way to hold it," he said, adjusting his grip. "When I rest it on my shoulder, it nicks my neck. Dangling it makes it bounce into my knees. And keeping it upright is exhausting. You'd think a sword this magic and old would come with a scabbard or something."

"Does he always complain this much?" Morgana asked me, cracking a smile.

I gave my tail a little wag and glanced at Arthur. "Usually more," I said. "But he's tired."

We all laughed, and Arthur shook his head.

"Did the Lady actually tell us where we're going?" he asked. "Or was she too busy making a snowman?"

"Hey," I said. "She saved us!"

"She's still a Fae," Arthur responded. "You saw what she can do."

"What? Are you afraid of powerful women, Arthur?" Morgana said, raising an eyebrow. "Because I'll be practicing again soon. And I don't want you having nightmares about it." She laughed, then stopped and turned to Merlin. "That is, when you think I'm ready."

"You've learned much," Merlin said reassuringly. "And Arthur has a lot to learn. Not all Fae are evil, my boy. Most aren't. They keep to their corners of the world and do their work without our knowing."

"Nivian's a good Fae!" I said enthusiastically. "She even brought you back from the dead!"

Arthur let the blade of Excalibur slip off his shoulder. "Why do you keep saying that?" he asked. "What does that *mean*, exactly?"

"Nosewise," Merlin murmured from the side of his mouth, "we'll ease him into magic *gradually*."

"Oh, um. My mistake," I said. "You weren't dead."

"Nosewise . . . ?" Arthur asked.

I looked around sheepishly. Morgana and Merlin were both subtly shaking their heads.

Then I saw something familiar in the distance.

"Wait! What's that?" I shouted.

"Don't change the subject!" Arthur said, but Morgana interrupted him.

"Oh, my stars!" she shouted. "It's our house!"

"What?" Merlin said, shielding his eyes from the sun. "Oh, how could I forget!"

"What is it?" Arthur asked. But the three of us had already left him behind. Morgana and I ran through the woods, crunching the snow under our feet. I looked back and saw

Merlin in a steady jog, faster than I'd ever seen him. Arthur picked up the heavy sword and took up the rear.

There it stood, nestled between two grassy hills that rose out of the side of the mountain: a brick-and-beam house fashioned just like the one we'd had in the woods so far away. The walls were made of rough-cut stones, and the roof was stacked with fir branches. A covered chimney peeked out from the top.

"It looks just like our old house," I said, turning to Merlin.

"Well, it should." He grinned widely. "The same man built it!"

"Really?" Arthur asked, coming up behind us. "What builder makes houses back home *and* on Avalon?"

"It wasn't just any builder," Merlin said fussily. "It was me!"

Arthur looked between him and the house. "You did it?" he said in disbelief.

"You picked up the stones and stacked them on top of each other?" I asked, as mystified as Arthur. I'd never seen Merlin lift anything heavy in my life.

"I had magic to help," Merlin said sourly. "I'm a wizard, not a barbarian."

"Forgive me, Master Merlin," Morgana said. "But how could you have built a house and not remember it?"

Merlin looked quite annoyed with the three of us. "I built this residence when I lived here. When I wasn't much older than you two!" He pointed at Arthur and Morgana. "Talk to me in sixty years and see what *you* remember."

"I don't think I'll ever forget this," Arthur said, hefting the magic sword.

"Me neither," I said, glancing down at my new Asteria.

"Nor I," Morgana said, shaking her head. "This has been *insane*."

"Well," Merlin said, "you haven't gotten old yet. Some mornings it's a struggle to remember my own name." He laughed and walked to the front door of the house. It was cold outside and it would be wonderful to get in and start a fire. Merlin grasped the iron handle and turned. *Rattle!* It was stuck. "And now I see I've forgotten my keys. I must have left them somewhere in the last sixty years." He turned and peered at us. "I hope all of you can forgive me that." We laughed, and I wagged my tail happily. It was so good to be together again.

"Perhaps a ghost hand spell to trip the lock?" Morgana suggested.

"Wonderful idea," Merlin answered her, and raised his staff to the knob.

"Wait!" I shouted, running between Merlin and the door. "Let me try, please! My Asteria is powerful here."

Merlin smirked and looked at me proudly. "Let's see what you can do." He stepped away and joined Arthur and Morgana behind me.

I breathed a happy sigh and considered the wide-paneled door in front of me. I settled my Mind's Nose on the spell I thought best and found an easy Certainty.

I love being with my family.

Blast! A spell of shock broke the door into four separate parts. The stupid door crumbled off its hinges and fell to the stone floor. I wagged my tail ferociously, very pleased with myself.

"That's one way to do it," Merlin said, and the others patted my head as they filed in.

The house was dusty, cold, and in disrepair. But Merlin, Arthur, and Morgana sighed with relief to be indoors again. Arthur rested Excalibur on some hooks he found on a wall, and Morgana and Merlin set to starting a fire in the hearth. I stood in the doorway, watching them.

"Nosewise," Morgana said, warming her hands by the newly lit fire, "aren't you going to join us?"

"Yes, my boy!" Merlin called, sitting down in an old stuffed chair. When his body hit the cushions, dust puffed out from every inch of fabric. Merlin coughed and waved his hands. "Come in—*ack!*—it's cold!"

I wagged my tail, barked happily, and joined my three loved ones in the warm house in the hills. Arthur scratched my ear. Morgana kissed my snout. And Merlin laid his hand on my back as I sat on the floor beside him.

Chilly wind blew through the open door frame, but I looked at it happily.

All my life, I'd hated doors.

But now I knew how to open them.

Author's Note

I'VE SPENT A LOT OF TIME CONSIDERING THIS QUESTION: "WHAT is the theme of *The Wizard's Dog?*"

My first book, *The Bully Book*, was about the power others have to shape your identity, and the difficulty of defining yourself.

My second book, *The Zoo at the Edge of the World*, asked what kind of relationship humans should have with animals and whether we had the right to control them.

After thinking about it for a long while, I believe I finally discovered the profound theme of this book too.

Dogs are the best.

They just are. Dogs, in my opinion, are the greatest things humans have besides each other. For the last 50,000 years, dogs have been by our sides as protectors, helpers, advisors, and buds.

My dog, Bowser, is one of my closest friends. He was my inspiration for Nosewise and dutifully sat next to me every day of my writing, providing comfort and support. I hope that you, dear reader, have a dog like that in your life. If you don't, there are plenty of wonderful animals in shelters right now, literally this very second, waiting for their chance to have a happy home.

I'd like to thank everyone who has helped me get out the message on the beauty of dogs. That includes my excellent editor, Pheobe Yeh, and her clever assistant, Elizabeth Stranahan. Nicole Gastonguay, whose art direction of this book was awesome, and Dave Phillips for his genius-level illustrations. My agents, Erica Silverman and Dana Spector, for their advice and support. And Jade, Nick, Matt, and Alyssa for helping me shape the story.

And Bowser, of course, for just being himself.

You can send questions and comments (or pictures of your pup!) to Eric at ekgwrites@gmail.com.

About the Author

ERIC KAHN GALE started *The Wizard's Dog* as a joke for his fiancée. He would tease that their dog, Bowser, was fascinated by the magic doors in their apartment that let him outside or delivered him food. It was a short leap from a silly impersonation to the spunky voice of Nosewise.

Eric is also the author of *The Bully Book* and *The Zoo at the Edge of the World*. He lives in Chicago with his fiancée and their nonmagical but entirely lovable dog, Bowser. You can find Eric on Twitter at @erickahngale and on Facebook.